A COOL KILLING

Stephen Murray was born in London in 1954 and educated at Whitgift School and Downing College, Cambridge. Married to a doctor, he worked for many years as a Chartered Surveyor before turning to writing full time. He lives on the edge of the Ashdown Forest in Sussex.

D1077762

STEPHEN MURRAY

A Cool Killing

FONTANA/Collins

First published by William Collins Sons & Co. Ltd, 1987
First published in Fontana Paperbacks 1989

Copyright © Stephen Murray 1987

Printed and bound in Great Britain by
William Collins Sons & Co. Ltd, Glasgow

Chapter One

'Would you see if you can raise Dr Swainson for me?'

'I'll try, Doctor, but when we bleeped him earlier we couldn't get any reply.'

Dr Angela Norman, tall, elegant, composed, waited calmly by the switchboard while the operator called her husband on the electronic paging device.

'There's still no reply. Do you want me to ring round?'

'Just try the lab, if you would, Mary. If he's not there it'll have to wait, I've a clinic in a moment.'

The girl rang a number on the internal phone.

'I'm sorry, Doctor. He was in earlier – I got an outside line for him.'

'All right, Mary. I expect I'll see him later. It'll wait till then.'

Smiling her thanks, Angela Norman turned away, crossing the echoing floor of the reception area with unhurried step, hands in the pockets of her white coat which flapped open to display a well tailored wool skirt and silk blouse. At her throat a single line of cultured pearls completed an ensemble which was as much a uniform and badge of rank as the blue dresses and coloured shoulder flashes of the nurses who passed to and fro.

Ovenden was an old hospital, a collection of buildings linked in no discernible order by a bewildering network of covered ways and lobbies. Somewhere at the centre was the original Edwardian cottage hospital, hidden among the accretions of the 'thirties and 'fifties, buildings now under-used as their functions had been taken over by the new district general hospital twelve miles away. The blood donor unit occupied a converted surgical ward, another had been adapted to form an old people's day centre. One or two remained totally empty, visited only by those who had lost their way, probationers on their first day and patients' relatives confused by the illogicality of the site. Gradually the hospital was regressing to its Edwardian origins, serving a local population who came for a short stay to have their babies in the small maternity unit, to various outpatient clinics, or for a longer, final stay in the geriatric ward.

With the unconcern of long habit, Dr Norman wended her way through the labyrinth of corridors, out into courtyards, through covered ways, past the maternity unit to a single-storey block of creamwashed brick, with a sign beside the door which said LADY ANSON MEMORIAL BUILDING. Beneath, the ubiquitous blue signboard of the health authority said, in stark and unconscious irony, *Family Planning and Venereology*. Dr Norman pushed open the door and went in.

'Do you think it's cold enough for crumpets?'

'Definitely. Crumpets would be perfect. Also Madeira cake and Darjeeling.'

'It's not the same, though, having them in summer. And without a fire. You don't think we ought to have scones instead?'

'Not at all. Crumpets will be fine. Don't worry about it.'

'But I want to get it right.'

Alec gave her a little hug. 'You will. You always do.'

'I wish I could get used to your friends, all the same. I try too hard to get things right, then I invariably make a mess of it and feel I'm letting you down, and all the time

I'm not coming over as me, if you know what I mean. I wish you hadn't seemed so inoffensive when we met.'

'That was my method. Not bad, eh? It usually works.'

'Maybe, but I don't particularly like to be on the receiving end of it. I suppose it's what makes you so good at your job.'

'Ah. Perhaps you'd like to come along and tell the Superintendent that. He inclines to the view that first impressions are generally correct and has been known to refer to me as the wettest thing in the force outside the underwater branch.'

'Oh, Alec. Surely not.'

'Actually, yes. In an audible aside to one of the Woman Police Sergeants he happened to have his eye on at the time. Should we make ourselves presentable, do you think?'

Diana sat up and refastened the buttons of her blouse. Alec watched her with a lazy, humorous turn to his mouth which she had grown to recognize as a sign of contentment. It was barely two months since Diana had accepted the invitation to move into Alec's flat, and looking back, she marvelled that she had had the perceptiveness to agree. She might so easily have been deceived by the outward camouflage and missed the delight of exploring the subtle and intelligent person within. At first it had been a series of jolts when she found that Alec was a policeman, already, in his early thirties, an inspector in the detective branch; that he held a decoration – this she learned from a friend, for Alec never mentioned it – from his time in the Army on a short service commission; that he relaxed to the sound of Gregorian chants; and that his circle of friends included the sons and daughters of people she was used to reading of in the papers, and who held Alec in genuine, if wary, respect. Later, Alec took her to the Hall and she met his parents. By then she was less easily surprised and it seemed somehow only consistent that his father should be a retired general and High Sheriff of the county.

From wondering what she was doing spending her time with an upper class twit she had passed swiftly to wondering what on earth he was doing spending his time on her. In this she did herself less than justice, for Diana herself was both clever and well-regarded and her parents, academics, were themselves eminent if not blue-blooded. Alec had watched with some amusement the evolution of her attitude towards him, and thought them to be a far more likely couple than Diana could yet see. For all his outward diffidence on casual acquaintance, Alec had a high opinion of his own judgement and it gratified him to watch Diana pass through the stages of conversion from sceptic to disciple. He valued her highly, however, as he valued the content she had brought him amid the harsh demands of his career.

Later, as they sat with their guests, college friends of Alec's, buttering crumpets and chatting inconsequentially, Alec acknowledged his good fortune. The fruits of a successful career – financial reward, a well-known name, maybe a knighthood – were still distant and uncertain, yet here and now there was little he desired which he had not got. The flat, with the elegance and proportion of the country house of which it had been a part, the outlook over gardens – no less pleasant for being shared – and countryside, his friends, Diana, even the fact that there were still goals to strive for added to his feeling of conscious content.

It was shattered by the telephone bell. Diana glanced at Alec, who shook his head, but when she answered the ringing it was for him, and despite his impassive expression as he listened to the call she knew it was work.

'Yes,' he said finally. 'I'll do that. Half an hour. Right.'

'Work?'

''Fraid so. Sorry to break up the party, but I'll have to go.'

'But you're not even on duty today,' Diana protested.

'Mm. All the same. Sorry.'

'Will you be long?'

'Can't say. You know how it is. Some chap's gone missing at the hospital; probably nothing to it, but being Sunday only Henry was in and he's gone home with 'flu. You stay,' he added to the others. 'Don't waste the rest of the crumpets. If someone chooses to go wandering off there's not much we can do, after all.'

At the police station, just off the sleeping Sunday high street, Alec found a detective-constable writing up his notes at a counter where an avuncular desk sergeant was intent on the Sunday paper.

'Sorry to trouble you, Mr Stainton. Inspector Griffiths thought he'd better take his 'flu home with him, then of course as soon as he'd gone we got this call from the hospital.'

'Right-ho, Jim. 'Afternoon, Andy. Shall we go into my office and you can tell me what's what.'

The young constable, still looking over his notes, followed Alec through into an inner room and took the offered chair. Alec sat on the side of the desk to reduce the formality of the situation.

'Well, sir, it's like this.' The detective-constable, who was probably no more than four or five years younger than Alec himself, looked innocently youthful in jeans and T-shirt. His translation from the uniformed branch was painfully recent and he was anxious to get everything right.

'All we got to start with was a call from Ovenden Hospital to say one of their consultants couldn't be traced, he was supposed to be in the hospital yesterday and nobody'd seen him, then he never went home either yesterday evening. Then he should have been back at the hospital this afternoon for a case conference or something and didn't show up, so by this time they were getting anxious and thought they should mention it to us.'

'Who was it who rang?'

'Hospital secretary – a woman called Miss Carmel. She wasn't quite sure what to do, but thought we ought to know.'

'Not very promising. You can't lose a consultant, after all. If he's missing, presumably it's by choice and there's not much we can do about it. Nothing from traffic?'

'No, sir, that was the first thing I checked. But his car was at home, anyway; he lives close enough to walk to the hospital, so that seemed to be out.'

'And you went down there?'

'Yes. Really, just so that they could see we weren't bored by it all.'

'Good. Who did you see?'

'Well, the secretary, of course, the one who rang us. One of the junior doctors who normally works with Dr Swainson – that's the chap that's missing. Then I went along to see Swainson's wife. She works at the hospital too, but she's kept her maiden name, Dr Norman.'

Alec nodded patiently. 'How was she taking his absence?'

'Well, much as you'd expect. I mean, anxious, puzzled, kept telling me she couldn't imagine where he'd got to. Not actually very worried, perhaps – yet. Last saw him on Saturday morning and so far as she was aware he was on his way to the hospital. Tried to reach him later in the morning but without success and says she didn't try very hard because it wasn't that important.'

Alec pondered, kicking at the leg of the desk. 'Pick up any undercurrents?'

The young detective-constable thought for a moment. 'Not really, sir. I mean, there didn't seem to have been any rows, the wife's anxiety seemed straightforward enough. She must realize it's quite likely he's just gone off for a weekend with a bird. So far as anyone was concerned he had just gone astray and it had finally got inconvenient enough for them to get on to us.'

'What do you think we should do?'

'Me, sir?' the constable looked startled at the question.

'Yes. What would you do if you were in my shoes?'

'I don't think there's much we can do, sir, is there, except make a note of it and wait for him to turn up?'

Alec smiled. 'Quite so. So let's do that. Perhaps tomorrow you and I can have another little trip out to Ovenden and see if anything else has come to light. Do you like crumpets?'

'Crumpet, sir? Why, yes, I – '

'Crumpets. Plural. With butter and jam. I think it's time I went to see if there are any left. Goodbye.'

And that, thought Alec as he drove home, was a waste of time. But he was wrong. In the morning when he climbed the steps and pushed open the swing doors of the police station it was to find the place in a state of near-panic. He stood bemused a moment while people scurried to and fro with worried expressions like anxious chickens, then the desk sergeant from the day before emerged from an inner room and caught his eye.

'Thank heaven.'

'What is all this?'

'It's that consultant that went missing up at the hospital. They've found him.'

'Fine. Why all the fuss? Where did they find him?'

'In the fridge.'

'What?'

'In the refrigerator,' the sergeant repeated grimly. 'In the hospital mortuary of all places.'

'Dead?'

'He's dead all right. I should think he's probably frozen solid.'

Well,' Alec said soberly, 'it's a remarkably thoughtful place to die, wouldn't you agree?'

Chapter Two

Alec stared at the clock on the wall and tried to concentrate on the Superintendent's voice. The clock said twenty-five past ten. Very nearly two hours since the discovery of the body of Dr Swainson in the mortuary refrigerator at Ovenden Hospital, an hour and a half since Alec had entered the police station. In that hour and a half there had been no lack of activity, but little of it seemed to have been to much purpose. Any moment now the hospital would ring back asking why no one had been sent round, and all the time whatever might be learned at the scene was growing more elusive as new events blurred recollection, changes in the weather effaced physical clues, rumour mingled imperceptibly with truth. Alec had little doubt that they had a murder on their hands. The other possibilities – someone stumbling on the body of Dr Swainson dead from a heart attack and conscientiously placing it in the mortuary drawer, subsequently being too upset or absent-minded to tell anyone, for example – seemed highly improbable. And then, in a hospital, where people had such a matter of fact relationship with death . . .

'. . . and so in the circumstances – ' he dragged himself back to the pompous voice of the Superintendent – 'you'd better make a start and I'll take over the reins as soon as I can arrange it. You'll report to me, of course, at every stage. I shall expect to be kept fully in the picture. I'll speak to the ACC directly. He'll appreciate that this is only a temporary measure. Now, have you got all that?'

'Yes, sir.'

'Good. Well, you'd better get down there, lad. You mustn't hang around where a homicide is concerned. It's been too long already.'

'Yes, sir. Quite so.'

'I'll try and look in later in the day, if my meeting at the Home Office finishes in time.' Alec looked at the clock again. The minute hand gave a little click and moved on another division. 'Is that quite clear?'

'Yes, sir, quite. Thank you.' Alec put the phone down with relief and sat for a moment marshalling his thoughts, before rising briskly. The phone started to ring again as he left the room. He ignored it.

Out in the front office some of the commotion had died down, but there was a air of anticipation that reminded Alec of examination day at school. Heads turned to him as he came through.

'Hospital on the phone again, Mr Stainton,' the desk sergeant said. 'I put it through.'

'Tell them we're on our way. And Jim, is Andy Johnson in? I'm going down there and I'd like him with me.'

'He's in the canteen, sir,' one of the WPCs volunteered.

Alec turned to her. 'Would you fetch him out for me? Tell him to get a move on. He can have another cup of coffee later. And Jim – ' he turned back to the sergeant. 'I don't suppose anyone's put the scene of crime team on to this yet? Get on to them and have them meet me down there. Doctor, too. Ah, Andy. Set? Let's get moving, then.'

Ovenden Hospital was set on the edge of the town, its grounds merging pleasantly with adjacent fields and insulating it from the housing estates. Detective-Constable Johnson preserved a diffident silence during the short journey out, being indeed rather in awe of this elegant and youthful inspector who, whether his reputation was

14

as a dilettante or as a brilliant whizz-kid, undoubtedly stood out from the normal run. Opinion in the station inclined to the whizz-kid view, not least since it conferred a reflected glory on them all, and Alec himself did nothing to discredit the opinion. Johnson was very conscious that today both of them were new boys – his first murder inquiry, Alec's first in charge – and was anxious that neither of them should blunder. Certainly the Inspector seemed cool enough, but still, a murder . . .

'I think we'll take a low key approach,' Alec broke the silence. 'No sense in getting carried away with our own importance, so we'll let other people do the talking and the running around so far as we can, and we'll just act as blotting-paper and soak it all up. Would you mind very much taking notes?' Andy, to whom the taking of notes was an everyday fact of life, said no, he wouldn't mind.

Turning in between brick pillars, they followed the direction signs through a warren of roadways to what seemed to be the main entrance, and parked in a 'doctors only' slot. At the the reception desk, the girl barely raised her head at the two young men, one slight and well dressed, the other heavier and in the inevitable jeans and denim jacket, bending her head again to write in a register. Eventually she straightened up and looked at them in polite enquiry.

'Detective-Inspector Stainton,' said Alec quietly. 'And Detective-Constable Johnson.'

The change in the receptionist's manner was comical. She looked beyond them in what Alec recognized as the instinctive search for someone older and more senior which so often greeted him when he introduced himself. Johnson shifted uncomfortably, and Alec hoped he would keep his head. Standing on one's dignity was usually a mistake, he found, and he didn't want it to get in their way today of all times. He contrived to look competent and unruffled as the girl lifted a receiver and pressed the buttons for a number, her eyes still assessing the two men.

'She'll be with you in a minute,' the receptionist said, putting the phone down. 'You can take a seat if you like.'

'Thank you.'

While they waited for the hospital secretary, Alec established the routine of the reception desk and switchboard. During the day they were manned by Mary, who was on duty now, or another girl, Maureen, while at night calls were taken by the porters. Not much went on at night at Ovenden Hospital, it seemed, and calls and visitors were few. Telephone calls in were not logged, merely put through to the relevant extension, while all outside calls had to come through the switchboard. It was hardly the most modern of systems, Alec thought, and must be diabolically frustrating and a great waste of time. It was, however, a good way of keeping tabs on people using the hospital phone for private calls. Alec was on the point of asking about the weekend when there was a clack of heels on the tiled floor and he turned to greet the hospital secretary.

Josephine Carmel was a compact, highly groomed woman in her mid-thirties, with a reserved but not unfriendly manner. Alec noted with some surprise the absence of wedding and engagement rings, for Miss Carmel's attractive figure and finely sculpted cheekbones would bring her as much admiration as most women could wish for, surely. For an administrator whose patch had been invaded by unexplained death she seemed remarkably self-possessed, but there were signs of strain in the fine lines at the eyes and mouth, while something about her make-up suggested that she might have been crying not too long ago.

'Inspector Stainton?' she looked from one to the other

of them queryingly. 'My name is Josephine Carmel. I'm the hospital secretary, the chief administrator here. I rather thought you might send someone sooner.'

The tone was one of polite surprise rather than reproof and Alec responded in kind.

'I'm afraid your call rather caught everyone on the hop. It happens on Monday mornings even in police stations. I'm sure you must have wondered what had become of us.'

The tiny lines round Miss Carmel's mouth turned down as she registered Alec's diffident manner.

'Perhaps we could have a brief word in your office,' Alec continued, 'and then we'll ask you to show us where Dr Swainson was found.'

'Of course. Will you follow me?'

'Now,' said Alec when Miss Carmel had ushered them to the visitors' chairs in her office, 'I'm afraid we've only heard the barest of outlines so far of what has happened. Would you mind very much going through the story so far, so to speak?'

Miss Carmel bowed her head. She sat with her chair sideways to the desk, though whether this was out of a courteous wish to minimize formality or to show her shapely legs to advantage was not apparent. Alec waited while she gathered her thoughts.

'Dr Swainson is – was – a consultant here, or to be more precise he shares his time between Ovenden and the district general hospital. He is a haematologist, that is, he is concerned with disorders of the blood, and as such has both an outpatient unit and a small laboratory here. The lab should really have been transferred to the district general when it opened, but Dr Swainson is to some extent a man of habit, and besides, he lives quite close to the hospital, so he has so far resisted attempts to move it from Ovenden, and actually spends the bulk of his time here.

'His wife, Dr Norman, also works here, with a clinic in family planning and venereology. Dr Norman spent a good part of Saturday here, but her husband should have been here all weekend.' She looked up. 'That is rather unusual, of course, for someone at Dr Swainson's level, but it was his way of working. Well, on Saturday one or two people tried to get in touch with Dr Swainson. One of the SHOs – Senior House Officers, that is – ' Alec nodded – 'and also, I believe, Dr Norman, tried to get a message to him. He was not to be found. That is not too unusual, and you understand that a consultant does not clock in with a punched card. He is to a great degree his own master. No one tried to reach Dr Swainson very determinedly. It can be difficult to trace someone in a place like this, even apart from the possibility that he had popped out to do some shopping, say. And none of the matters was that urgent.'

'He would have an electronic bleeper?'

'He would, but he might not have it with him. That would be perfectly legitimate on his part; I believe Mary said he did ask for an outside line earlier in the morning, so presumably he was here then, but that was the last time anyone seems to have spoken to him.

'Well, by Sunday afternoon people were beginning to wonder more seriously where Dr Swainson was, and the senior nursing officer rang me at home. I live within a short walk of the hospital, and I came over. That would be about half past two on Sunday, perhaps. I set in motion a more systematic search, ringing round the various places Dr Swainson might be, including the district general hospital and of course his home. Dr Norman told me that her husband had not been home at all since he left for the hospital on Saturday morning and it was this, really, that prompted me to ring your police station. I did not say as much to Dr Norman, but I was beginning to think that Dr Swainson must have met with an accident of some sort. This young man – ' she indicated Johnson, sitting quietly to one side, notebook in hand – 'came round. We chatted it over, and decided to wait on events. I believe your people were to make some inquiries about road accidents and so forth.' Miss Carmel paused, and licked her lips with a nervous gesture.

'Today, a firm of undertakers came to remove from the mortuary the body of an elderly woman who died at the end of last week. They collected the key from the receptionist, with my permission. They are a local firm and have frequently been here on similar business. They drove over to the mortuary, let themselves in and went through to the inner room where the refrigerated compartments are. These are like drawers, let into the wall behind a door. There are six of them. Our mortuary is very little used, Mr Stainton, and in consequence we only make use of one drawer normally, the bottom left. It saves having to label the outsides. The corpses are themselves labelled, of course, so there is no chance of confusion. Anyway, the undertakers' men knew our routine and went straight for the bottom left drawer. Unfortunately – or fortunately, I don't really know how I should describe it in the present circumstances – the porter was new to Ovenden, and had put the body of the dead woman in the bottom right-hand drawer. When the undertakers' men opened the bottom left, it should have been empty.' Miss Carmel paused, with a fine sense of timing. 'It wasn't. It contained a body, that of Dr Swainson. Of course,' she went on more briskly, 'they didn't know who it was, but they did know that something was badly amiss. I don't know if you are conversant with procedure in mortuaries, Mr Stainton, but bodies are not placed in the refrigerated compartments fully clothed, as this one was. And this body was not . . . composed. The men acted very sensibly. One of them stayed in the mortuary, the other came across and spoke directly to me. I went back with him, and of course – ' she paused and swallowed – 'I saw at once that the body was that of Dr Swainson. I had the mortuary locked. I hope that was the correct thing to do. Then I called your station. And now,' she let a slight emphasis fall on the word, 'here you are. That is all.'

Behind Alec, the scratching of Johnson's pencil continued a moment, and he waited for it to stop.

'Thank you, Miss Carmel. That was very lucid indeed.' He paused.

'You mentioned that the body of Dr Swainson was not, ah, composed. I wonder if you could elaborate a little? If you wouldn't mind.'

Miss Carmel licked her lips. 'There isn't much room in a mortuary drawer, Inspector, so anybody who is in one must be stretched out full length. But in this case the b . . . Dr Swainson was lying half on his side, and hunched down towards the front of the drawer.'

'Was he in head first or feet first?'

'Head first.'

'Is that usual?'

'No. The head would normally be nearest the door.'

'Do you imagine he was placed in the drawer in this rather clumsy way by someone who wasn't familiar with the normal method of doing things?'

'It's . . . possible.'

'But not very likely, you think? What else might account for the disorder?'

Miss Carmel hesitated, reluctant to put into words the possibility which she was almost sure this young detective must have considered already.

'He might . . . that is, if he had been alive when he was put into the drawer, then his position would . . . would be consistent with an attempt to get out.'

'Is that what you think happened, Miss Carmel?'

'Yes.' The fine profile turned and she looked Alec in the eyes, then turned away again, as if still contemplating mentally the struggles of a dying man.

'There was no obvious wound, you see. And then, it wasn't just the position of the limbs. The hands, too, the fingers were raw and they'd been bleeding. He must have been scrabbling at the sides of the compartment, he would have been desperate to get out. You can't, of course. They're locked by a handle on the outside. You'd never get out unless someone let you out.'

'From which you deduce . . . ?'

She turned to him again. 'That someone put him there deliberately. That he was murdered.'

'Or that he got in there to see what it was like, and couldn't get out,' Alec said easily, 'or perhaps that someone put him there thinking he was dead when he wasn't really, or that he died elsewhere and damaged his hands some other way. Perhaps the experts will be able to tell us which of these possibilities is true. Tell me, Miss Carmel, what would be the temperature in one of these refrigerated compartments?'

'They're not really refrigerated, more chilled. The temperature stays a few degrees above zero, about four degrees, I think. I'd have to check.'

'Cold enough to cause death if you were in there long enough.'

'I suppose so. You'd have to ask one of the doctors.'

'And Dr Swainson was in there perhaps from Saturday morning to Monday morning. Well, that's another one for the experts.' Alec glanced at his watch. 'I wonder if we could go and have a look, Miss Carmel. I'm afraid this is all going to take you from your work for some time.'

'I think you may be right,' said Miss Carmel wryly. 'So let's make a start.'

They followed her back down the corridor and out through the reception area. After the stark interior it seemed slightly indecent that outside the sun was shining warmly and the birds singing. Somewhere not too far distant was the sound of machinery, and a smell of fresh cut grass drifted towards them. Alec thought what a splendid day it would be for lying in the shade with Diana, and how they must do that soon, take a picnic and spend a whole day being sixteen and in love in the midsummer countryside, before they found the chance had passed them by.

'It's a fair walk, I'm afraid,' the secretary was saying. 'The mortuary is rather on its own and understandably tucked away.'

'That's quite all right,' Alec said courteously, and turned to smile encouragingly at Andy Johnson trailing awkwardly behind them. 'I wonder,' he continued, 'whether we should have left a message with the receptionist. I've asked some of our people to come over, you see, what we call the scene of crime team.'

'Mary will send them over. Or ask them to wait till we return. She's very efficient.'

The mortuary was an unassuming building in dull red brick, something like a Methodist chapel of the less inspired sort, set back from the tarmac roads but with a driveway wide enough for ambulances and hearses to turn in. Miss Carmel produced a key from her pocket which she inserted in the lock, at the same time turning a brass handle dulled with neglect. The door swung inwards and they entered.

At first Alec thought they had indeed strayed into a

chapel, for a small table, which might have been an altar, with an embroidered cloth on, faced four or five rows of chairs. To one side was a less formal area with armchairs and a low table bearing a selection of periodicals. To the other side acoustic screens separated off a small administrative area with desk, telephone and office chair. Behind this a wide door in the far wall led to an inner room. As he followed Miss Carmel towards this door, Alec glanced at the desk. It was a functional affair of metal tubing with a plain top covered with grained plastic, bare of papers or files. He bent closer to look at a score in the plastic top. It ended in a small puncture, and there was a trace of something darker on the fibres of the cloth where they had been torn and exposed. He straightened and followed Miss Carmel.

'Isn't this door usually locked?' Alec asked in surprise.

'No. There are only three keys to the outer door, and anyone who has one of those normally needs access to the bodies, anyway.'

'And the refrigerator?'

'No. No locks. Just good strong catches with handles on the outside. Perhaps . . . well, perhaps after this the hospital will take a stronger line on security. I don't know. It's worked well up till now, but I suppose that's no great recommendation.' She smiled wanly at him. 'It just means no one's tried to abuse the system before.'

Now that they were in the inner room of the mortuary, Miss Carmel seemed to hang back a little, and merely indicated the far wall with a clumsy gesture. She had turned rather white.

'I wonder if you'd like to wait in the ante-room?' Alec asked politely. 'Perhaps you would, too, constable.'

Miss Carmel hesitated, unsure whether Alec was implying she needed watching, or merely being considerate.

'I generally find it helpful to take my first look round on my own,' Alec explained. Miss Carmel smiled briefly and turned to leave. Johnson raised his eyebrows to Alec, who merely gestured him to follow the secretary.

He shut the door after them and turned to consider the room. It was, as he expected, stark, functional and old-fashioned. The painted walls, mustard to waist height, beige above, reminded him of the corridors of his prep school. He glanced up at the windows, three on each side, long, thin casements set horizontally just below the ceiling. They had been designed to open, but from where Alec stood they seemed well sealed with age. He reached his arm up against the wall. The tip of his palm came several feet below the bottom sill.

In the centre of the room was a bare table, long and narrow, with an enamelled top. Beyond was a deep ceramic sink with long extensions to the taps to enable them to be turned on and off with the elbows. A clean roller towel hung alongside.

Reluctantly, Alec turned his attention to the end wall and the bank of six doors, like those of domestic refrigerators, which faced him. Two of them must conceal dead bodies; behind four the compartments should be empty. He made for the middle door in the bottom row and pulled it open.

Behind the old-fashioned door the compartment stretched blackly away. Alec examined the floor, pulling it forward on runners till it projected into the room like the drawer of a filing cabinet. It was chill to the touch. Turning his attention to the door, he found, as Josephine Carmel had said, that it fitted flush to the front edge of the compartment. A rubber sealing strip ran round the inside, otherwise it was smooth. The catch on the outside was simple but strong; there would be no chance of bursting the door open from the inside, and Alec tried to imagine the nightmarish panic which would seize anyone who found himself trapped in one of these compartments. He slid the drawer home and shut the door.

That left two drawers in the bottom row, and he moved across to the right-hand one. Deliberately, he turned the handle and opened the door. A swathed mass lay in the gloom within, and Alec slid the drawer out. It ran heavily but easily on its runners, revealing to the harsh fluorescent lights a bound head and a shrouded body. Pinned to the shroud, a label said simply 'Florence Annie Timms' with a date, that of the previous Friday. Alec gazed at the wrapped form, then deliberately slid the drawer back.

Taking a clean handkerchief from his pocket, Alec wrapped it round the spindle of the left-hand door handle and, with some difficulty, for it was inclined to slip, undid the catch and swung the door open. A pair of shoes confronted him, and he noted calmly that they were leather soled, and quite new. The soles were quite clean and dry, but the edges of the uppers were scuffed, the leather roughened and white, and on the inside of the door jamb were traces of brown substance that might be shoe polish. Choosing his spot carefully, Alec grasped the underside of the drawer and slid it heavily out. He stared down thoughtfully at the form of Dr Geoffrey Swainson, consultant haematologist, where it lay before him.

Dr Swainson was dressed for weekend work in sports jacket and cavalry twill trousers, but the clothes were rucked up awkwardly, so that the woollen shirt had pulled from the waistband of the trousers, and both jacket and trousers were stained and damp. There was a smell of vomit, and a trickle of the stuff lay in the creases round the mouth. The hair was matted and a hairpiece had been pulled loose, lying with gruesome rakishness across the forehead. Alec gazed down at the features, shorn of a consultant's dignity, noting the tracks of tears on the cheeks, the one open and the one closed eyelid, and thought there could be no bleaker evidence of the vanity of human activity. Angry, he shook his head to clear it and turned his attention to the rest of the body, registering the hands, torn and raw, clutched close to the body as if the consultant, in despair at his fruitless attempts to escape, had hugged them to him, crying, as he slipped into the chill of death.

Scuffling and muffled voices reached him from the outer room; there was a tap on the door and Johnson put his head round.

'Scene of crime people are here, sir. And the doctor.' His glance fell on the body, and he faltered.

'Right,' Alec said. 'Would you ask them to come in? And take Miss Carmel back and stay with her. I'll be over directly.' Johnson withdrew, and Alec heard his instructions relayed to the visitors. The door opened again, and a very dark, stout man of Alec's own age entered, followed by an older man, emaciated, with a serious expression.

'Peter,' Alec greeted the younger man. 'Forgive me for teaching you to suck eggs. There would seem to be a good possibility that the body could have been brought here already dead, otherwise, usual cause, time, and so forth. I'm sorry, I suppose you probably knew Dr Swainson?'

'I've worked with him on occasions. In fact, I spoke to him only on Thursday. Didn't expect to meet him again in here.' The doctor spoke with the healthy spirits of the medical man.

'David.' Alec turned to the older man. They were equals in rank, and Alec was careful to accord the scene of crime inspector the respect which his experience demanded. 'Thanks for coming so quickly. You probably saw there's a tear in the top of the desk outside, looks quite recent. And have the windows been opened, all that sort of thing. And all the other things I haven't even thought of. There's another body in the right-hand drawer, but probably nothing to do with the matter in hand. Still, if you wanted to have a look? I expect they'll be wanting to take that one away as soon as they can, and perhaps we'd better not be too obvious about checking it out, in case there are relatives . . . you know how it is.'

'Leave it to me. Anyone else coming in on this one, or is it yours?'

'Mine for the time being,' Alec smiled. 'But not for long, if the Super has his way. So I must mind my p's and q's. I'll be over in the main block when you've done.' He left them to their tasks and with a nod to the scene of crime team waiting in the outer room went out thankfully into the sunshine and made his way slowly back to the main entrance.

Chapter Three

Josephine Carmel sat at her desk, trying to work through some routine papers as if a detective-constable were not seated opposite her and a consultant were not lying hunched in a cold mortuary drawer a few hundred yards away. Johnson for his part was sensibly concentrating on his notebook, seemingly making the occasional entry or alteration. He looked up as Alec came in.

'Now, Miss Carmel,' Alec began. 'I expect you realize that until things are cleared up we shall have to stay at the hospital, certainly for a day or two. Could we, do you think, have the use of a room and a desk somewhere so that we can be out of everybody's way? And, er, perhaps we could come to some arrangement over our people using the canteen here? If not, I dare say . . .'

'No, that's all right. I'll make sure the canteen staff will admit them. They, er . . . ?'

'They'll pay in the usual way, yes, of course. Thank you.'

Miss Carmel stood up, then seemed to recollect herself and sat down again. 'I was just going to arrange a room, but I can do that over the phone.'

'Oh no, please feel free to come and go as you wish. I do beg your pardon. When I asked Detective-Constable Johnson to return with you it was a matter of convenience, not by any means a way of suggesting you could not be allowed to be on your own.'

The secretary gave him a searching look, and Alec thought again that here was a woman well suited to authority, an admirable woman in more than one sense, and a very attractive one too – in a mature sort of way, he added hastily to himself. When she had left the room he turned to Johnson.

'I fancy we should be prepared for this to take some time. Assuming Swainson was done away with deliberately, there could be dozens of people in a place like this with a motive for getting rid of him, and most of them would have the means and the skill to hand as well. What a frightening way to go, though, don't you agree?'

Johnson shuddered. 'It's like one of those dreams you have as a kid, sir. Where you're confined somewhere and the walls start closing in. I've never liked being hemmed in, myself.'

'We'd better hope the doctor can tell us he was dead before he got in there, but on the face of it it seems unlikely.'

'I've arranged for you to have the old physiotherapy unit,' Miss Carmel said, rejoining them. 'It's a separate block, a little way from the main buildings and not too far from the mortuary. We haven't used it for a few years, I'm afraid, they all go to the district general now, so it'll be a bit musty, but there's plenty of space and I'm having it cleaned up and some furniture put in. It'll be ready in an hour or so, if that's all right with you.'

'That's very kind of you,' said Alec. 'It'll be a help being on our own, and it'll keep us out of your hair, I hope.' He smiled at her. 'Now, what I have to do, as I'm sure you realize, is begin gathering information about Dr Swainson. The scene of crime people will find all there is at the mortuary, so perhaps I could ask you to start by telling me what sort of person Dr Swainson was. Was he popular, for example?'

Miss Carmel looked disenchanted. 'You want me to . . . gossip, that's what it amounts to?'

'Just so,' Alec replied blandly. 'If you wouldn't mind.'

The secretary crossed to a filing cabinet and sorted through one of the drawers till she found a manilla folder with a number in the top corner. It was marked 'Staff – In Confidence'. She took it back to her desk and leafed through it, refreshing her memory, but made no attempt to offer it to Alec. Finally she closed it and crossed her hands protectively over it.

'Dr Swainson is – was – forty-six. He's a consultant haematologist, as I told you, and has held the post for five years. He is regarded as a very good doctor, well thought of in his field, and is often asked to speak at conferences and so on. He spends three days a week here, together with the occasional weekend when he likes to catch up on lab work.' She looked up. 'Incidentally, I have not told his wife of his death yet. I shouldn't want her to hear by accident or from some malicious gossiper.'

'Thank you for reminding me, Miss Carmel. I'll ask one of our WPCs to see to it, if I may use your telephone?' Alec dialled 9 for the receptionist while Miss Carmel looked studiously out of the window, and asked for an outside line. When the desk sergeant at the station answered, Alec confined himself to asking for a WPC to be sent out to the hospital directly, making a mental note meanwhile to check whether Mary was able to listen in to outside calls.

'Please go on,' he said, putting the receiver down and turning to the secretary again.

'That's about all there is. Dr Swainson is a very competent amateur pianist, and he and his wife frequently perform at hospital concerts and so on. She is a cellist. She works here too, but I told you about that.'

'Actually, Miss Carmel, you've told me nothing that I couldn't have found from reading that file, have you?'

'I'm afraid I couldn't let you have access to the personal

files of staff. They are hospital property, and confidential,' said Miss Carmel coolly.

'Nevertheless,' said Alec, letting the rebuke lie for the time being, 'what I want is something more personal, more subjective, if you like. Did people like Dr Swainson?'

'I really don't think . . .'

'Miss Carmel, I should be grateful if you would answer my question.'

The secretary's face flushed darkly and Alec wondered if he had overdone it.

'If you would be so good?' he added neutrally.

'I think . . .' she began, then shrugged and smiled. The flush faded. 'I suppose you are right. This is an exceptional situation and of course I want to do everything I can, everything I properly can, that is, to help. Well, as to whether he was liked, it depends who you are talking about. He was generally liked by the other medical staff – the doctors – because they respected him, and he was not an inconsiderate colleague. He was less popular with the nursing staff, rather talking down to them, if you know what I mean. Of course, as a haematologist he didn't come into contact with them as much as if he'd been a surgeon or something, and that may have accounted for it. He never became really easy with them.'

'Did he involve himself in emotional relationships? A hospital is full of women, after all.'

'No, he . . . That is, a hospital is always full of rumours, Inspector. There is hardly anyone who is not involved in something like that, if you listen to rumours.'

'And there were rumours about Dr Swainson?'

'As I say, it would have been unusual if there were not. I hear the rumours, and I treat them as just that. Gossip. No more.'

'Did you yourself – ' Alec sensed a heightened tension

in the secretary and saw that her knuckles were white where they were clasped over the file. 'Did you yourself know Dr Norman and her husband socially?' he finished, changing his question in mid-sentence. Was it imagination, or did the tension slacken marginally?

'Yes, I knew them moderately well. We shared an interest in music and enjoyed the occasional evening together.'

'And did they seem a well-suited couple?'

'So far as one could judge. I am not married myself, Inspector, so there will be nuances of behaviour between married couples which I have no experience of interpreting. I should have said they were as contented as . . . as you might expect.'

Alec considered this inconclusive assessment. 'There was no reason to think Dr Swainson was in poor health? I just wonder whether there is anything in particular our doctor ought to look out for.'

'So far as I know he was perfectly healthy. His wife, of course, would be the person to talk to in that connection.' Miss Carmel rose from her seat and went over to the window, gazing out with her back to Alec.

'I don't know much about these matters, Inspector, thank God. But I assume we now have a murder enquiry going on. I just want to know, because it is going to affect the hospital considerably. For a start, the press . . .'

'There's no point pretending that the death of Dr Swainson looks at all natural, Miss Carmel. Beyond that, you will understand that I would rather wait on the findings of the pathologist and the scene of crime people. I think perhaps if you were to proceed on the assumption that a murder inquiry will be set up, while refraining from using the word, you would not be far wrong.' He looked at his watch. One o'clock.

'Well, you've been most helpful, Miss Carmel, and I'm

sorry we have to trouble you in this way. The best thing I can do now is leave you to your work and make a start on my own, if you could show us where to set up shop? Don't worry if it's not quite ready, we'll make a start anyway.'

Alec followed the secretary with some relief that he could stop being polite and start getting the inquiry under way. He was very conscious of the hundred and one things which needed doing the first day of an operation like this – the press statement, the widow to be comforted and discreetly questioned, the Superintendent who would shortly be emerging from his Home Office meeting, ready to intervene in the case. He thought ruefully of lunch, and put the thought behind him. He only hoped that the borrowed office would run to an electric kettle. Coffee, in copious quantities, was clearly going to be a necessity at every stage of the inquiry.

Three-quarters of an hour later, Alec put down the phone and sat back in his chair. A half-eaten ham sandwich lay on a plate beside him, and he took it up gratefully, but the cold coffee with its creamy skin he pushed aside in distaste. The WPC had reported in and been immediately despatched to the Swainsons' house to break the news of her husband's death to Dr Norman, with instructions to stay with her as long as seemed decent or profitable. A brief statement had been composed and read over the telephone to the local papers, sufficient not to satisfy them but to justify Alec in withholding further comment until the picture was clearer. He had rung the police station and warned them to readjust duty rosters so as to leave himself, Johnson and the WPC free, and had got through to the county police headquarters to find that the Superintendent had not yet emerged from his Home Office meeting.

'Probably reading them a paper listing all their faults

and how they should set about putting them right,' said his informant. 'Pity the poor buggers. It'll teach them not to invite him again for a while.'

Finally, he had rung the university and left a message for Diana. It was an unsatisfactory arrangement, for he badly wanted to speak to her, but, he told himself briskly, it served to keep home and work apart and today that was particularly desirable.

There was a knock at the door and Johnson, who had stationed himself as a sort of PA in the outer room, put his head round.

'The doctor's here, sir. Can I send him in?'

'Thanks, Andy. Don't let anyone disturb us for a bit. Ah, Peter, have a seat. Can we get you a cup of coffee?' He nodded to Johnson. 'Make that two. I seem to have missed out on the last one. Now,' as the door shut behind the detective-constable, 'where do we stand?'

The doctor settled himself in his chair and leant forward.

'First thing is, he was alive when he went into the drawer. Now, don't ask me why he should have obligingly climbed into the thing, or whether it could have happened by accident, because that's your field, not mine.'

'Could he have done it by accident? I don't know much about mortuaries, though I fancy I'm beginning to learn.'

'Personally, I should say not, but as I say, I'm a layman when it comes to that side of things. I mean, you'd have to set about it pretty deliberately to get yourself into one of those drawers, and then manoeuvre yourself backwards with your hands. And shut the door afterwards, don't forget. His feet were at the door end. So if you're asking me could it have been done by accident, or even as a form of suicide, I'd say not in a million years. Now, cause of death, that's probably asphyxia. You noticed the vomit, well, he'd have choked on that. As to the time, you'll have to wait till the pathologist has a look at the stomach contents in the post-mortem. Personally, I think he was quite fortunate to go by choking, if it speeded things up for him.'

'He would have died anyway?'

'Oh yes, if he was in there all weekend, no question.'

'Even though the temperature was above freezing?'

'Absolutely. Bear in mind that he could hardly move in there, and obviously he couldn't take any hot food or drink. Oh yes, I doubt if he'd have lasted till Saturday night. Simple hypothermia – exposure, if you like. His only chance would be if someone came to remove the other body, or a really thorough and clever search was organized as soon as he went adrift. Failing that, he'd had his chips, and he would have known it. Hence the panic, and the damaged hands, and the vomit which as it happened took him out of his misery.'

There was a tap at the door and Johnson entered with coffee in paper cups. 'County HQ came through, sir. Just to tip you off that the Super's on his way home. Do you want me to stall him if he rings?'

'No, put him through. Thanks, Andy.'

'I suppose,' Alec continued when they were alone, 'almost anyone in a hospital would know the consequences of imprisoning someone in a mortuary drawer? What you tell me about hypothermia, that'd be common knowledge in a place like this.'

'Oh yes, I should say so. Among the medical and nursing staff, at any rate. Probably among the domestics and ancillaries, too. They're very hot on keeping up with their medical education.'

'So you wouldn't put someone in there as a practical joke? No. And anyway, why should Swainson submit to it? Had he struggled with anyone? The scars on the fingers . . . ?'

The doctor hesitated. 'Better ask me that when we've done a proper PM. The nails are pretty much messed about, there could be anything under them. On the face of it, there are no obvious signs of a struggle, but . . . ask me later.'

'Thanks. Well, you've given me the "how" of death in one sense, with the asphyxia. But the other "how", how he got into the drawer, seems to be a total mystery.'

'Sorry about that,' the doctor said easily. 'Actually, I shall be quite interested to learn how it was done myself, when you've found out. OK for now?' He got up. 'They'll take the body, if that's all right with you, and I'll get the PM set up for this evening. You've rung the coroner?'

'Blast, no.'

'Leave it with me, I'll check that one. They may have done that when they discovered the body. By the way, did anyone certify him dead?'

Alec stared at him. 'I never thought to ask. I got the impression that they found him and immediately locked everything up and rang us.'

'Just a thought. Leave it with me. There's identification, too, but I can probably do that. Ah well, you've got your hands full. Oh, by the way, I had a quick look at the other body, Flossie Whatsit. All seems to be in order.'

'Are they taking her away too?'

'No, there's some hold-up, I don't know what, they're leaving her till tomorrow. Anyway, I'm off. David's outside, champing at the bit. Shall I shoot him in?'

'If you would. Thanks, Peter.'

The doctor went out and there was muttering from the other room, then the spare form of the scene of crime inspector stalked in.

'Alec.'

'David.'

'The boys are just clearing up, and I've told the doc he

can have the body, so far as I am concerned. We haven't finished the outside and the surrounding area yet, but I thought you'd like a bulletin. Everything in hand so far?'

Alec grinned. 'If it isn't it's not for lack of good advice. If the doc was telling you to watch out for things I've missed, feel free.'

The older man relaxed in his chair. 'I'll let you know. We're all glad you've got this one, so nobody's going to hesitate to throw you a lifeline if they see you beginning to sink.'

'That's very kind,' said Alec, taken aback.

'Hr'm. Now, what have we found? Well, nothing of very obvious help. You mentioned the windows, so I'll start with those. They've not been opened since the coronation, I should think, and no sign that anybody's tried recently, either. Fingerprints. Plenty on the fridge door-handles, except the one where the body was found – that's been pretty well wiped. We think, but it's a bit of a guess, that it was opened with gloves rather than, say, a handkerchief. Inside, Swainson's prints all over the place, all the parts he could reach, all much smeared and some overlaid with bloodstains. Oh, the door to the other fridge, the one with Florence Timms in – someone's had a wipe at that handle too, but not a very thorough one. Swainson's prints are there. On the handles to the door to the inner room and the main entrance door, all sorts of prints, all recent.'

'Top ones will be those of the secretary who let me in.'

'Right. Those are there earlier, too, overlaid by some-one else's in between. Possibly the undertakers' men, if I've got the story right. Prints on the desk, Swainson's, including a palm print. May have been leaning on it to write, the position fits, and the dust's certainly been disturbed in the last few days. So much for prints. What else? Usual things in the pockets. No convenient notes signed by the murderer arranging to meet Swainson in the mortuary. Hm. Brown shoe polish on the inside of the drawer, same as that on Swainson's shoes – we'll get a proper analysis just to be sure. Now, on the drawer itself, where it slides out on runners, we picked up some fragments.' He rummaged in his briefcase and brought out two or three plastic bags. 'These – ' he held one of the bags up; minute fragments of thread were just visible within – 'these are threads from Swainson's trousers, as might be if he was climbing up or being lifted in.

'These – ' he held up a second bag – 'are some sort of very thin plastic. Should get a better idea when it's been to the lab, but my guess is very thin rubber gloves. Surgical gloves, maybe, though that's jumping to conclusions.'

'The tear in the table?'

'Recent. Ink on the fibres where they're exposed. We'll check that against the ink in Swainson's fountain pen.'

'And the direction of the tear? Someone ripping at the tabletop in frustration or anger, perhaps?'

'Could be,' the inspector said cautiously. 'Not inconsistent, but I wouldn't like to put it more strongly than that.'

'That the lot?'

'Not quite.' He held up the third bag. 'Key to the outer door.'

'Good Lord.'

'Didn't expect it?'

'I certainly didn't. On the body?'

'No, it was down by the side of the desk in the ante-room. As if it had been knocked off by accident, perhaps. Have you traced who had the keys over the weekend?'

'Not yet. One of the many things I've not done, David. But I could have sworn the secretary said none of the keys were missing. Well, that ought to give us a lead, anyway.'

'One more thing. You know there was quite a lot of grass in there, one way or another?'

Alec smiled. 'I brought some of it in on my own shoes, I expect.'

'Right. Well, in one place – and this was a real piece of detective work. One of the young chaps. They have such sharp eyes,' he said wistfully. 'Anyway, in one place the grass has definitely been brought in on a high heel. A ladies' shoe.' He sat back in satisfaction and watched Alec's reaction. 'And not as recently as this morning.'

'A high heel?' Alec heard again in his mind the clack of the secretary's heels as she crossed the reception area to meet them. 'You could identify it?'

The inspector looked a little crestfallen. 'Well, to tell the truth, I don't know. There's no impression on the floor, of course, which is tiled and as hard as they come, and no convenient muddy footmarks. It was the way the grass had actually been compressed which told us about the shoe, but it was just in the one place and there's nothing else to compare it with. Of course, if you got us a shoe we could try and match it, but . . . '

'I'll see about that one. Anyway, a high heel narrows it down a little. It isn't every woman in a hospital who's allowed to wear them, after all.'

'Well, as I say, we haven't quite finished outside, and if anything comes up I'll give you a ring. Keep the mortuary locked, of course, in case we have to come back to check anything.'

'I'll do that. I don't think they use it much, and I'll make sure everyone who wants to get in comes through me.'

'I'll leave you to it, then.'

'Thanks. Any minute now the Super's going to be ringing me up wanting to know the whole story, so what you've told me should keep him going for a bit.'

'Not to worry. Even the Super's not God.'

'I know, but nobody seems to have told him that. That the lot?'

'For the time being. I'll let you know if anything fresh comes up. Maybe I'll pop in tomorrow if I get the chance and just see what's happening.'

'I'd like that. Thanks, David.' The phone rang at Alec's elbow. 'Guess who. I'll see you. Thanks again.' The older man nodded amicably and the door closed behind him as Alec picked up the receiver.

'How about another cup of coffee if you can tear yourself away?'

Andy Johnson sat on the edge of his desk swinging his legs, and looked round guiltily as Alec entered. In Johnson's chair sat WPC Jayne Simmonds – Jayne 'with a Y' as she had politely informed Alec on her first day at the station, and had been puzzled when he merely murmured 'Y indeed?' An attractive girl of twenty-two or -three, her fair hair tied neatly back as regulations demanded, she had time for everyone and as a result was resolutely pursued by every policeman under the age of thirty, married or not, and by several of the older men, too, who persuaded themselves it was only right they should keep a fatherly eye on her. All these attentions she took good-humouredly in her stride, accepting with equal calm the younger men's confidences and the older men's complaints about their wives, all the time pursuing her career with careful determination. She was a good policewoman, and Alec couldn't begrudge Johnson the pleasure he took in the fact that she had been assigned to the case.

'Spare me a moment, Jayne?'

She rose obediently and followed him into his office. Johnson turned resignedly to the kettle and wondered when some real detective work was going to be done.

'Now. You've been to see Dr Norman.'

'Yes, sir.'

'Like to tell me about it? Your own impressions, as well as what she said.'

WPC Simmonds crossed her legs modestly and leafed through her notebook, laying it open on her lap for reference if need be.

'Well, sir, she's rather a formidable woman in her way. I gave her the usual bit about how I had some news about her husband and could I come in, and she went pale, but very composed, and said had he had an accident? I said yes, I was afraid he had, and she said, "He's dead, isn't he?" and so I said yes, I'm afraid so, and she drew her breath in very sharply as if trying not to sob. I kept quite a close eye on her, sir, and she really reacted just as a loving wife would. Then she said, "How did it happen?" and I said, like you told me to, that we didn't quite know yet but he'd been found in a very strange place; and she asked me where, and I told her.'

'How did she react to that?'

'She seemed not to understand me. She said of course they had taken him to the mortuary if he was dead, and I explained it again and she said, "Oh, Geoffrey," and got up and walked about and sat down again, just like someone would who's not used to letting go emotionally. If she was acting, sir, she really was very good. Then she did start to cry, and I just stayed with her. In the end I said was there anyone I could ask to come and be with her, but she was quite calm by then and said no, she wanted to be on her own to get used to the idea, she couldn't take it in, and was I sure he was really dead? Well, I said I was afraid there was no doubt. Then I left.'

'So far as you are concerned she had no idea her husband was dead till you told her, and then she reacted just as one might expect?'

'That's right, sir. Though she must have guessed it was a possibility, by that time.'

'Well, I'm going to have to go and see her, of course. I think it might be better if I did that straight away.'

'She did say she'd rather be on her own for a bit, sir.'

'I know that. Which makes it a good time to go. You can't always be nice in the police force, Jayne.'

'No, sir.'

'Anyway, I shall want you to come with me.' Alec went through to the other room. 'Andy, I'm taking Jayne away for an hour or two, you'll be sorry to hear. Will you man the fort? And I've got to go to county HQ later. I'd like you to stay here then, so it'll be a late night for you, I'm afraid. Get yourself something from the canteen now, then you won't have to go later. I don't want the phone left for the time being. OK, Jayne with a Y, as soon as he gets back, we'll go.'

The Swainsons' house was a pleasant Victorian affair, once a leafy villa on the rural edge of town, now surrounded by the tide of later development but retaining its grounds, its laurels and its gravelled carriage drive. By Victorian standards it was not large, but by those of modern estates it was prodigal in its accommodation. Alec noted that it took them fourteen minutes to walk from the hospital. Perhaps familiarity might trim another two or three minutes from that time, unless there was some short cut of which they were not aware.

Alec was amused by the sense of inferiority which crunching conspicuously up a carriage drive tends to confer, aided in this case by a lengthy wait in the elaborate porch, which he spent examining the stained glass panels with which it was decorated.

When the door at length opened, he saw a woman of forty or so, on the tall side but without awkwardness, whose cool expression changed to one of disapproval as she registed the presence of the WPC.

'Good evening,' Alec said neutrally. 'My name is Stainton – Detective-Inspector Stainton. WPC Simmonds I believe you have already met.' He proffered his warrant card, which was ignored.

'I'm sorry to have to ask you one or two questions in connection with the death of your husband. May we come in?'

The cool expression hardened. 'You've chosen a very insensitive time to call, don't you think? I told this young woman I preferred to be alone to come to terms with . . . with my loss. I would rather you came back tomorrow, if you must come at all.'

Alec slipped his warrant card back into his pocket. 'I'm sorry to intrude, but I really do need to clear up one or two matters as soon as possible so that we can come to some conclusion about your husband's death.'

'It really isn't convenient now. You must leave me alone. Who is in charge? Tell him I will see you tomorrow. I don't want to talk to anyone tonight.'

'I don't think you understand, Dr Norman.' She blinked at the note of authority in Alec's tone. 'Your husband has been discovered dead in very unusual circumstances. It is not inconceivable that he has been murdered. I have been charged with investigating his death, and had assumed you would wish to help us clear the matter up as soon as possible. Now, may we come in, please?'

Dr Norman regarded them assessingly for a moment, then moved aside, holding the door to let them enter. In silence she showed them to a spacious sitting-room and gestured them to deep armchairs.

'All right,' she said, 'since you insist, I will help you as much as I can. But you really are being totally insensitive in coming here at this time, and if you try to browbeat me just because I am on my own I shall make sure your behaviour is reported to your superiors. I have several acquaintances in the more senior ranks of the police force.'

Well, at least we've got that gambit out of the way early on, Alec thought as he ignored the indicated armchair and opted for a more upright one that left him and Dr Norman on the same level. WPC Simmonds saw too late the disadvantages of the armchairs and sank uncomfortably lower and lower until she seemed to be sitting on the floor, her face meanwhile growing redder and redder.

'I'll be as brief as I can,' Alec said. 'I wouldn't trouble you at all if it were not absolutely necessary. WPC Simmonds has told you where your husband's body was found?'

'She told me something. It sounded totally confused and very unlikely, but I'm afraid the shock of hearing that Geoffrey was dead may have meant I didn't listen very clearly. Perhaps you can tell me the truth.'

Alec thought: This is like playing chess, and resisted the temptation to point out that he was the one to ask the questions.

'What Miss Simmonds said was quite accurate. Your husband's body was discovered in one of the refrigerated compartments in the hospital mortuary early this morning. How and when it came to be there we are trying to determine. Is there anything you can tell me that would shed light upon this?'

'Nothing. It seems totally mysterious. Are you saying that someone put Geoffrey's body in the mortuary without telling anyone? How had he died? You . . . you used the word "murder", Inspector. Surely you are not seriously saying my husband was murdered? Surely not. Who by, for heaven's sake, and why?'

'Well, it could have been some sort of accident, but murder is a possibility, I'm afraid, Dr Norman. So you see we have to treat this death very seriously indeed. Now, you last saw your husband . . . when?'

'Saturday morning. When he went into the hospital. He . . . he got up about seven – that was his usual time. He liked to take his time and be at the hospital about half past eight. I had a clinic later in the morning so I lay in for a while. We often used to have Saturdays like that. Geoffrey would bring me a cup of tea in bed before he went.' A muscle twitched in her cheek, and Alec noticed that her knuckles were white where her hands were clasped in her lap. He pressed on.

'He did that last Saturday?'

'Yes, I said so.'

'Then you went in later, and at some stage tried to contact your husband via the switchboard, without success.'

'I went in about a quarter to ten. I didn't try very hard to reach him. Mary – the girl on the switchboard – offered to try and track him down, but I was in a hurry and it wasn't important. I mean, he could have been just immersed in his work and not answering the phone. He was like that sometimes. It was rather bad of him, but he could get away with it.'

'What was it you wanted to speak to him about?'

'I'm not sure that's any of your business, Inspector.'

'I can't judge that until you tell me.'

'It was nothing important. I . . . I wanted to remind him that it was his sister's birthday soon. We usually go over to see her. I wanted him to keep the evening free, that's all.'

'And it didn't make you anxious, when he couldn't be found?'

'If I'd tried harder to get hold of him it might.'

'If you'd done that, he might still be alive,' Alec said, and wondered if that was going too far. 'And the next thing was that Miss Carmel rang you on Sunday afternoon to ask if Dr Swainson had been home. As a matter of interest, wouldn't you have expected him to sleep at home on Saturday night? The hospital is so close that it would be hardly worth having a room for him there, surely?'

Angela Norman hesitated. 'He could have come home, but he didn't. I mean, he often didn't, and he didn't last Saturday. He used to say that by staying at the hospital overnight he kept home and work separate. He was a man set in his habits, Inspector.'

'Is that the way you prefer to work, too?'

'I don't find it necessary to compartment my life in quite the same way. But then, I am not my husband. He was very good at his job, and he had the dedication that goes with that.'

'You use the past tense very naturally, Doctor.'

'What if I do? He's dead, isn't he?' She raised her eyes calmly to Alec's.

'Did Miss Carmel tell you she was going to contact the police?'

'No. She rang me to see if he was at home, but it wasn't until that evening that I found out that she had carried out a very extensive search for him. A young man came to see me. A detective-constable, apparently, though I must say he looked more as if he was on the dole. He wasn't very bright, kept asking me the same questions over and over. He didn't really seem to know what he was doing. All he succeeded in was making me very worried about Geoffrey.'

Alec was glad Johnson was not here to hear himself so dismissively spoken of.

'Inspector, you haven't told me how my husband died. Please tell me.'

Alec looked at her, noting the drawn skin around the eyes, the unnaturally bright pupils. 'I'm afraid I'm not going to tell you that just for the present, Dr Norman. The picture is far from clear, and we don't know quite how he came to be in the mortuary. I hope we shall soon.'

Dr Norman sat silently in her chair and Alec watched as tears gathered in the corners of the eyelids. Whether by habitual self-control or deliberate effort, Dr Norman seemed to take hold of herself and the tears remained where they were, unshed.

'Was your husband in generally good health? He wasn't under any sort of treatment, weak heart, anything like that?'

Dr Norman answered dully. 'He was always healthy. No, he wasn't taking anything. He slept well, without tablets, his heart was sound, and so on. Healthy people do die, you know, Inspector. It happens.'

Gradually the tears spilt from the eyelids and coursed silently down Angela Norman's cheeks. Alec watched in compassion and Jayne Simmonds struggled from her armchair to hold Dr Norman's hand with practised tenderness.

After a while the tears ceased and Alec said, 'I have to ask you this, though it's distasteful. Do you know of any grudges against your husband? Any reason why anybody should be . . . should not be sorry at his death?'

She shook her head.

'And you and your husband were on good terms?'

Dr Norman raised her eyes to Alec in reproach, and Jayne placed a gentle hand on her shoulder.

Alec said brutally, for there was no other way of saying it, 'Was either of you having an affair?'

The room seemed suddenly still. Alec watched the

sophisticated woman before him, her make-up barely streaked by her tears.

'I think you'd better go, don't you, Inspector?' she said icily. 'Geoffrey was a model husband. We've been married fifteen years. Now get out, please. I don't want to see you again. You're not fit to be a policeman.'

Alec rose. 'Thank you for speaking to us, Dr Norman. I'm sorry about your husband's death, and I'm sorry we had to trouble you. We can see ourselves out.'

Awkwardly, they left.

Chapter Four

'Nevertheless,' he said as they crunched down the drive, 'she didn't deny it.'

'And she didn't say she loved him. Only how long they'd been married. Calling him a model husband sounded a bit damning to me.'

'Mm. Would you say she was an attractive woman, Jayne?'

WPC Simmonds thought seriously. 'Well, speaking as another woman, and therefore not entirely objectively, sir, yes. A little too well turned out, if you know what I mean. But for a woman of her age, very attractive.'

'I agree. Speaking as a man, I should have thought that to spend Saturday night in bed with Dr Norman would be preferable to spending it on one's own in a hospital room.'

'Yes, sir. If he was on his own.'

'Constable Simmonds, you have a nasty, suspicious mind.'

'Yes, sir. If you say so.'

Alec pondered the matter as he drove over to county police HQ later that evening. It seemed likely that Dr Swainson had died sometime on Saturday, and that being so, he clearly had not been up to no good in some nurse's bed on Saturday night – not this Saturday night, anyway. But if he was in the habit of spending Saturday nights away from home, that probably suggested a longstanding relationship. How often had he actually used a hospital room? It was quite possible that he really was a dedicated and totally virtuous model husband who happened to prefer working odd hours. The theory of an affair certainly offered motives for murder to several of those involved – wife, lover, ex-lover now discarded, lover's husband, to begin with. Obviously the rumours which Miss Carmel had talked of must be followed up. If they could pin down more accurately the time of death, or rather, the time Dr Swainson had been placed in the mortuary drawer, then he could begin to sort out who had the opportunity and the means to commit the act. And, if anyone had opportunity and means and also had motive . . . but he suspected he was letting optimism run away with him. Then there was the matter of the high-heeled shoe. Well, that suggested a woman had been in the mortuary over the weekend, but there were plenty of women in the hospital, even if you excluded those who weren't allowed to wear high heels – and even they had off-duty hours. Then, where had the grass come from? That one was easy. The verges to the paths and drives had been recently cut, he could recall that the cuttings had spilled on to the tarmac in places and he had kept to the centre of the path to avoid them. But when precisely had it been done? If it was Friday, for example, it was no help. But supposing it had not been cut till Saturday? Or Sunday? Damn. He had meant to trace the mortuary key that had been found by the scene of crime people, and it had totally slipped his mind. Any copper on his first day at work would think to do that, and he had let it be squeezed out by other matters less urgent. Ah well, it was too late to do it today.

County police headquarters was a large, modern building in a parklike setting, much at odds with the cramped accommodation and antiquated appearance of most of the local stations. Among Alec's colleagues it was known as Whitehall Palace, not only for the expanses of Portland stone with which the ratepayers had tastefully clad it, but also because of the exalted positions of its inhabitants.

Alec went straight upstairs and made his number with the Superintendent's assistant, a young uniformed constable who acted as flag lieutenant and zealously filtered out those visitors his superior did not wish to see. So far as this visit was concerned, Alec was expected; indeed, he was given to understand that he had been expected for some time and that he was the direct cause of the Superintendent's loved ones being deprived of his presence. Alec went in.

'Stainton,' the Super greeted him abruptly. It was his habit, and, Alec suspected, his affectation, to be curt and by so doing to seem businesslike and authoritative. Despite this, he was perfectly capable of being curt at great length, so that less rather than more business was actually achieved. To Alec, the Superintendent was a fact of life, made bearable by the knowledge that if all went well Alec's own star would shine far brighter than the Super's in due course. This knowledge was probably shared by the Super and did nothing to soften his manner.

'I've been having a word with the ACC,' the Superintendent went on. 'He wants to see you. He's stayed specially, so you're keeping him waiting. He agrees with me that you should report to me at every stage of this case. You know the system: you can't be given charge of a homicide case. You're too junior in rank, and even if it was allowed, it would hardly be in your own best interests. However, provided you realize that, you may as well stay on the case now you've made a start. Got your report?'

'It's being typed,' Alec said truthfully, having left the task to Johnson for the evening. 'It'll be on your desk tomorrow morning.'

'I hope so. I haven't had the results of the PM yet, I

understand it's still in progress. This is a copy of the Scene of Crime report. You can keep it,' he said magnanimously.

Alec took the smudged carbon and noted with amusement that it had originally been addressed to himself, with copy to the Superintendent. That was good of David, even if bad for the old man's ego.

'What have you done? Got statements from the main characters?'

'Not yet. I've spoken with some of them, including Swainson's wife.'

'Dr Swainson's wife,' said the Super, emphasizing the title, 'has had a terrible shock. Don't harry her.'

'You know her, sir?' Alec guessed.

'They've dined with us before now. She's a very well respected lady and more than one senior officer will be keeping an eye on this case on her behalf. That is another reason why it is desirable that I should seem to take a back seat in this enquiry, to minimize the personal element. You may count yourself lucky that it gives you the chance to help with a homicide so early in your career. Now, you're keeping the ACC waiting. Make sure that report is with me first thing tomorrow, and every day from now on. That's all.'

As he rose two more floors in the lift, Alec marvelled that a man with a hide as thick as the Super's should nevertheless be such a good detective as his record showed him to be. He was just a sod to work with, Alec decided, and understandably resentful of people like himself.

The outer room of the ACC's office was empty, and the inner door stood ajar.

'Ah, Alec.' The Assistant Chief Constable was a mild-mannered man who at first sight gave the impression of diffidence. Indeed, he was reticent, and known closely to none of his colleagues. Nobody remained long in doubt, however, about his competence. He was known to command the ear of very important people in the wider world, and was tipped for a Chief Constableship within the next year. Alec privately regarded the ACC as something of a model for his own career.

'Have a seat. How're you getting on?'

'Slowly, sir, I'm afraid. I seem to have very little to show for the day so far.'

'Not to worry. It takes far more time than one could imagine, until you try it. Are you happy in the job, that's the point?'

Alec said, 'I think so. I've a fair idea of the way I would like to set about things, and other people have been a great help with advice and so on.'

'Well, you must always ask for advice if you need it. I've decided to let you take the front seat in this investigation, Alec. You'll report to the Superintendent in the usual way so that we can keep tabs on things, but in essence it'll be your own show. Do you think you can handle that?'

'Yes, sir. Thank you very much.'

The ACC took out a battered pouch and began to fill his pipe. 'I don't want you to feel this is make or break. It's early for you to be handling a murder enquiry. Some might say too early. If you get bogged down and someone has to come in to help you out, it'll be no disgrace and you'll still have had the experience. Of course, I don't say that will happen, and if you should pull it off it'll be a very large feather in your cap. You may expect to be criticized at some levels, and people will say it's too much responsibility too soon, but don't let that throw you from doing things the way you think best. If the criticism gets too hot I'll handle it, and if need be I'll take the decision that the Superintendent should take over more detailed control. All right?'

Alec smiled. 'That's fine, sir, I'm very grateful.'

'Good. Your father well?'

'Very, sir, thank you. We were at the Hall a week ago and he was very fit.'

'I must give him a ring. I imagine he'll be involved in this ministerial visit?'

'I think he's been asked to meet them off the train, sir. There's some question of a guard of honour.'

'Lot of fuss for a tourist trip for a cabinet minister. Well, go and get some sleep and make a fresh start tomorrow, and keep the reports coming in. I've come across the Swainsons before. It's a terrible thing to happen to anybody and we must clear it up as soon as we can.'

'Yes, sir. Good night.'

The note on the kitchen table said simply, 'Casserole in oven. I am not asleep.' Alec ate the casserole hungrily, sopping up the gravy with a piece of bread, conscious that it was late and he must make an early start in the morning.

The bedside light was on, and Diana breathed peacefully, eyes closed, on her side of the bed. Alec undressed and slid in beside her. As he reached for the light-switch she stirred and rolled over sleepily.

'Is it a big one?' she murmured.

'Yes.' Alec found his voice breaking slightly with excitement. 'Yes, it's a very big one. And I'm in charge.'

'Lovely, darling. Night-night.' Diana was already asleep again, and Alec flicked the switch and settled happily against her.

In the morning, when Alec unlocked the door of the physiotherapy building which was now his office, his

—

thoughts were clearer. Sitting at the desk, he listed on a sheet of paper the priorities for the morning, including the people he must interview. The afternoon he left free, guessing it would fill itself soon enough. Reaching for the telephone, he put through a call to the police station and asked for Jayne Simmonds to be sent out again, in plain clothes this time, and to be taken off other duties for the time being. Then, consulting a list of internal numbers, he dialled the secretary's room, glancing as he did so at his watch. It was just half past eight.

'It's Detective-Inspector Stainton here, Miss Carmel. Sorry to disturb you so early. I wonder if you could arrange for Mary, the receptionist, to come over. As soon as possible, really. She's in this morning? Right. There will be other people I have to see, but I'll try not to trouble you too much.'

Detective-Constable Johnson came in as Alec put down the receiver, and hastily sat at his desk in the outer office. Alec could see him through the half-open door quickly threading another sheet of paper into the typewriter. Alec picked up the phone again and dialled nine for the switch-board. An unfamiliar voice answered and gave him an outside line.

Diana answered first ring, in her brisk morning voice.

'Only me,' Alec said. 'Sorry I had to dash out before you were awake. Look, I'm going to keep very odd hours, I'm afraid. Did you get what I said last night about the case, or were you asleep?'

'I got it. Just. I'm glad for you, and itching to hear about it. Don't worry about me, I'll cope till you get this sorted, I dare say.'

'Don't bother about meals for me. I can always get something in the hospital canteen.'

'Don't be silly. I'll leave something on every evening, something that'll keep hot. I can always have it next day if you don't get back at all. I know what canteens are like. You will be back here to sleep?'

'Hope so. Can't guarantee it, though, I'm afraid. Take care.'

'You too, darling.'

There was a knock at the door and Johnson poked his head round. 'I've done a cup of coffee for us, and the receptionist's here. Do you want her to come through?'

'Please. How's that report for the Super coming along?'

'All done. You want me to take it over when you've read it?'

'If you would. I'll do that first, then you can take it while I have a chat with Mary. Ask her to wait a moment or two, if you would.'

Mary Whinbush was a sandy-haired, freckled girl in her early twenties, not striking to look at, but with an easy and intelligent manner which would be an asset in her work. Nevertheless, she betrayed some signs of nervousness as she sat down opposite Alec, and he smiled encouragingly at her.

'Look, Mary, what I'm doing is gathering what I would call background to this matter of Dr Swainson's death. Later, I may ask you to make a formal statement, but for now I want you just to let me ask you questions as they come into my head, and talk as freely as you can. Now, you are the main receptionist here?'

'That's right. I share the daytime rota with Maureen, but I'm really supposed to be in charge.'

'And you've been here . . . ?'

'Four years.'

'Like it?'

'I do. It's not such a big hospital, so you get to know people and there's quite a friendly atmosphere. And being on reception, of course, you're involved in everything that's going on.'

'So you see people who come in, patients and visitors and suchlike, and you also take calls and get outside lines for people.'

'That's right. I get pretty busy sometimes, but generally you can just about cope.'

'And you like to keep abreast of everything that's going on.'

'It's not that, exactly, I mean, there's not really time to be properly nosey, it's more that you can't help picking things up.'

'Quite so. Now, I'm going to be nosey myself, Mary, and I want you to bear in mind that I have to be if I'm to clear up what happened to Dr Swainson. I want you to tell me what you know of him. What he was like, who he did and didn't get on with, whether he rang his wife when he was going to be late home, whether he was conscientious at his work, whether he used the hospital phone to ring his stockbroker – anything at all you know about him. It's a bit of a liberty to ask you to gossip about someone, especially now he's dead, but it's because he's dead that I want you to do it. All right?'

Mary nodded.

'OK, away you go.'

Geoffrey Swainson had been, so far as Mary was concerned, friendly and polite but not really forthcoming. He always greeted her when he came past the desk and said good night if he passed it again at the end of the day, though as often as not he would go out via another of the hospital's innumerable entrances. When he asked for an outside line he spoke to her by name, but on the other hand his politeness had remained at the same level over the four years she had been in her job, never growing into familiarity. Mary believed he was much the same with his colleagues, never, for example, joining them for a lunch-time drink except on those occasions when someone was leaving or celebrating an engagement, when he would punctiliously attend for half an hour, buying a round of drinks, good-natured but not matey.

Was he the same with male as with female colleagues, Alec asked.

Mary hesitated, and it was clear that she was reluctant to slander the dead. She thought – knew, rather – that there were some women with whom he had been on much closer terms. There had been affairs. He was not a hospital Don Juan, that would have been totally out of character. However, in the four years she had been at the hospital Dr Swainson had certainly had at least three affairs: one with a radiographer, another with a staff nurse, a third with a junior doctor.

So although Dr Swainson was quite reserved with most people, there had hardly been a time when he was not involved in an affair?

Yes, but they had been quietly conducted and, so far as one could tell, amicably ended. Mary doubted if the hospital at large had been much aware that they were going on.

Alec thought of the rumours mentioned by Miss Carmel and fancied Mary might be mistaken on that point. The last affair had ended – when?

About six months ago, when the young woman doctor had gone to a new post in another district.

And since then, nothing?

Nothing that Mary had noticed.

Might he have started another affair of which Mary was unaware?

He might, but she thought it unlikely. Even if it was with someone outside the hospital, the nature of Mary's job meant she would probably come to know about it.

But her general impression was that the affairs had

been discreetly and amicably conducted? Just so. And Dr Norman?

Mary didn't like Dr Norman. The dislike was not expressed in so many words, but she made little effort to hide it, and clearly had fewer reservations about 'telling tales' where Angela Norman was concerned. Dr Norman was inclined to be bossy and to stand on her dignity, particularly where other women were concerned. She was not particularly popular with other doctors, and so far as Mary knew had never been associated in any amorous way with anyone at the hospital. On the other hand, she did keep in touch with a friend, an older man, who sometimes came to take her out to lunch. There was no sign that it was a sexual relationship especially, but there Mary was merely surmising from her own observation. Mary's conclusion, for what it was worth, seemed to be that Dr Norman found some prurient satisfaction in her family planning and venereology clinics, and had less inclination for personal indulgence.

All of which, Alec thought, backed up the idea that she was hardly head over heels in love with her husband, but scarcely formed a case against her for murder. Besides, he had encountered before couples who looked elsewhere for sexual satisfaction while remaining totally and surprisingly committed to each other by both habit and inclination.

He asked Mary about the events of Saturday morning when she had been on duty. Dr Norman had wanted to get in touch with her husband at some stage?

Yes, about ten or so. He wasn't to be found and she hadn't pursued it.

So Mary didn't know whether Dr Swainson had been in the hospital that day?

On the contrary, he had rung through earlier asking for

an outside line, so he had certainly been in then. Somewhere between nine and half past, that might have been. No, she couldn't tell what number he had subsequently dialled and no, she never listened in to conversations, although it was possible. Alec thanked Mary politely and released her.

Showing Mary out, Alec found that WPC Simmonds had arrived and was amusing herself by leafing through the copy of the report to the Superintendent which Johnson had carelessly left on the desk. She looked up with a touch of guilt and smiled uncertainly. Alec nodded her through to his room while he closed the door on Mary.

Out of uniform, casually but not sloppily dressed, there was no doubt that Jayne Simmonds was very attractive indeed. Alec was pleased to see that she had chosen her clothes carefully so as to be acceptable at most levels of the hospital community – neat enough for the upper echelons, not so formal as to intimidate those lower in the hierarchy.

'How do you feel about doing some general snooping for me?'

'Fine, sir. I haven't any CID experience, of course, but I'll give it a try.'

'Good girl. I'm probably very much at fault for taking you out of uniform, but we'll cross that bridge when we come to it. Look, I want you to spend some time in the canteen, in the rest-rooms, and so on, picking up gossip from the nursing staff in particular, and also from administrators, typists, secretaries and so forth. It'll take some skill. You may as well be fairly open about who you are and what you're doing, but keep it as informal as you can – be sort of off duty, if you know what I mean. Oh, and don't stick only to the women, if you think there's anything to be learnt from the men, especially the younger doctors. Play up to them a little. Think you can do that?'

She smiled. 'I can always try, sir.'

Privately Alec thought: I bet you can. 'Off you go, then. Come back after lunch, or if I need you before that, I'll send for you.'

Next, Alec put through a call to the police doctor.

'Beat me to it – I was going to ring you,' the doctor said when he heard Alec's voice. 'There's a report on its way to you from the pathologist, but it's going via county HQ. Do I understand the Super's running the case personally now?'

'No, you don't,' Alec said drily. 'But I fancy he wants to make it clear that I am acting under his guidance. Can you give me the gist?'

'Nothing dramatic. Death by asphyxia, as I said, probably some time on the Saturday afternoon. As to when he went into the drawer, the pathologist says Saturday mid-morning probably, not earlier. He's going by temperature changes and so forth. He's reluctant to be too precise.'

'Naturally,' said Alec glumly.

'Now, we looked for signs of a struggle, of course. Nothing under the fingernails, no bruises or anything. Looks as if he obligingly climbed up into the drawer of his own accord. Some women's hairs and a few traces of powder – David's got those now. Small stain on the index finger of the right hand. David tells me there was a fountain pen in one of the pockets. No traces of poison, no punctures in the skin, no obvious drugs in the blood or liver, though that's tricky unless we know what we're looking for. Um. He hadn't had sexual intercourse since his last bath.' A hint of distaste carried down the wire. 'And his last bath was none too recent.'

'How recent?' Alec asked sharply.

'Four or five days? At least. He didn't strike us as a very fastidious man where cleanliness was concerned.'

'Any chance of working out who he last slept with? Suppose we got some sort of candidate – could you check by cross-matching?'

'Can't be done,' the doctor said decisively. 'Sorry.'

'But it would have been a woman?' Alec asked neutrally.

'Right. No sign that he'd ever indulged in anything else. That's about it. We've run one or two other tests, nothing very likely. We'll get the results later for those, but I shouldn't hold out much hope if I were you. Do you want me to go over his medical record, if you can get hold of it?'

'That would be useful, though you seem to have ruled out all the convenient ways he might have died. I'll see if I can get hold of them, but I've a suspicion they'll be regarded as state secrets here.'

'OK, if you get stuck let me know. I might be able to have a quiet word with his GP, just to find out if there was anything.'

'His wife says not.'

'Well, she should know. Anyway, is that enough to be going on with?'

'Great. Thanks, Peter. I'm very much obliged.'

Alec put the phone down thoughtfully, then picked it up again and spoke to Mary on reception. Five minutes later there was a tap on the door and a young Indian in a white coat entered, followed directly by DC Johnson returning from county HQ.

'Dr Pritti,' Alec said, trying to give it some intonation that would make it not sound like 'pretty' and failing. 'Have a seat. Thank you for sparing me the time.'

'That is quite all right.' Dr Pritti smiled engagingly. 'I am happy to help.'

'You work with Dr Swainson, is that right?'

'I am his clinical assistant.'

'Could you tell me something about him?'

Dr Pritti, it transpired, was Swainson's assistant at Ovenden Hospital, and spent all his time there. His was most of the routine work of analysing samples, attending ward rounds where blood complications were involved, and generally acting as resident haematologist. He was able to call on Dr Swainson for advice, of course, and on the three days a week when the consultant was at Ovenden they shared the lab and an office. At the district general hospital arrangements were slightly different, as befitted a more major unit. There, Swainson's deputy was a senior registrar, next step down from a consultant, with a senior house officer as well, doing the more routine work.

Wasn't it unusual, Alec asked, that Dr Swainson should spend more of his time at the smaller of the hospitals?

Maybe, said Dr Pritti, but it was close to his home and for that reason he chose to do most of his research work at Ovenden. Much of Swainson's time was concerned with preparing papers for conferences, submitting reports to working parties, setting examination papers and so on, and it was easier, if slightly irregular, for him to make Ovenden his base.

What would happen now he was dead?

Well, the health authority could get a locum consultant to fill the gap while they advertised the post. In fact, they would probably ask Swainson's senior registrar, Dr Ingham, to take over on a locum basis.

Would Ingham be in line for the permanent post?

Dr Pritti put his head on one side and placed the tips of his fingers together.

'I believe not. In the normal course of events it would be so. However, Dr Ingham most unfortunately had a hiccup in his career when his wife was ill, and as a result has published little research. He had done well to get a senior registrar post, but it would be unusual indeed for him to be appointed to a consultancy. And he might now be regarded as rather old.'

'But he is younger than Dr Swainson, I take it?'

'By a few years only. The district hospital likes to think of itself as a dynamic hospital.' Pritti nodded to himself as if assessing the aptness of the word. 'Yes, a dynamic place. They will look for a man or woman – probably a woman – who is on the way up. Dr Ingham, I fear, has reached the plateau of his career. That is only my opinion, you understand. He is a good haematologist, too, so it is unfortunate.'

'Do you think he realizes how it will go?'

'He may do, if he admits it to himself. Before, he could blame his position on Dr Swainson. It was a case of dead men's shoes, if you will pardon the expression, with no chance of promotion in this district while Dr Swainson remained in post. He found it hard to take, I am afraid.'

Dr Pritti said this with some sorrow, and no apparent consciousness of having handed Alec a plausible motive for murder.

'Tell me, Dr Pritti, did you like Dr Swainson?'

'He was a very good haematologist, and easy to work with. I did not get to know him closely, but I liked what I saw, yes.'

'And his wife?'

'Dr Norman is a very charming woman, yes indeed. Again, I do not know her well. I fancy not many people do.'

Alec tried another tack, hoping it might be more productive than the last.

'Have you any idea what might have taken Dr Swainson to the mortuary on Saturday morning?'

'Oh, that is easy. He went to sign a crem form.'

'He what?'

'A cremation form. It must be signed by two doctors, usually the junior who was treating the patient and a senior. A woman had died on the geriatric long-stay ward, and Dr Swainson had to countersign the form. For that he would have to go to the mortuary and see the body.'

'And he did in fact sign it?'

Dr Pritti hesitated. 'Now, there is a mystery, I believe. I have heard a rumour that the form has been mislaid, and so they have not been able to take away the body. But it is not my department, I have only heard what is being said.'

'Quite. Now, on Saturday you yourself were where? At work?'

It seemed that Dr Pritti had been in on Saturday morning only, and then not for long. He had not seen Dr Swainson, and thereafter there seemed to have been little opportunity for him to commit murder, if his movements could be substantiated. Alec thanked him, and apologized for keeping him from his work. After the doctor had gone, Alec sat back in his chair and looked through his notes.

'Andy,' he called. 'I'm going up to the canteen for a bite. Hold the fort, will you? While I'm out you can make a start with checking the mortuary keys from Friday p.m. to Monday morning. Find out where they're usually kept, who took them out, and so on. Scene of Crime got one of them in the mortuary – find out which one that was, and when it was last seen. Should have done that first,' he muttered to himself, 'still, better late than never.'

Sitting in the canteen, a cup of coffee and a Danish pastry in front of him, Alec made out a fresh list of things to do. Dr Ingham's whereabouts should be checked out, if only to eliminate him from the list of possible suspects. Then there was Dr Norman. Her clinic should provide her with a solid alibi for Saturday morning, but it would have to be checked in detail. Then again, in view of Swainson's amorous proclivities and his habit of staying away from the marriage bed, was it really so certain that he had spent Friday night at home? The whole thing is complicated, thought Alec, by the fact that we don't know exactly when he went into the mortuary drawer. And, for heaven's sake, why? Even for someone he trusted he would hardly have done something so stupid as to climb up and allow himself to be pushed into his tomb. And if he had been rendered unconscious beforehand, why were there no signs of a blow, or an injection. Even a stroke, or a heart attack?

Alec finished the last cold dregs of his coffee. At a table on the far side of the room Jayne Simmonds sat with a group of nurses. A babble of laughter drifted across from their direction, and Alec hoped she was having better luck than he was.

Back at the office, DC Johnson was on the telephone checking the history of the keys. Mouthing that he would be back in an hour or two, Alec grabbed his jacket and left him to it. Probably, he thought, he should be sending Johnson to interview Dr Ingham while he himself stayed at the centre of things, but he felt the need to talk to as many people as possible personally about the dead consultant, in an effort to put together a picture of him which would point to a reason for his death. Perhaps also, Alec rationalized, I need to get out into the fresh air to clear the brain.

Chapter Five

The district general hospital was all that Ovenden Hospital was not: new, designed as a whole, bustling with life and urgency. The entrance lobby was an impressive affair with light wood panelling and a marble floor, and a plaque prominently displayed told that it had been opened by HM The Queen Mother only a couple of years before. Alec, remembering the delays and disputes which had kept the completed building notoriously empty for more than a year, smiled as he read the wording of the plaque, then made his way over to the reception desk and, showing his warrant card, waited while Dr Ingham was called on the bleep.

Roger Ingham was a small, tired-looking man in his early forties who welcomed Alec guardedly into a bare office and didn't offer him coffee. There was an air about Ingham which suggested a chip on the shoulder of some standing, though there was also a hint of smugness which might be of more recent origin.

'I'd like you,' Alec began, 'to give me your impressions of Dr Swainson, how you got on, what he was like to work with and so forth, and then I'll ask you some routine questions.'

Dr Ingham, it emerged, had not much liked Dr Swainson. He didn't say it in so many words, but then, Alec reflected, he hardly needed to. The consultant's reputation, it appeared, was not completely justified, and Dr Ingham thought it was based on no more than the fact that Swainson spent much of his time swanning about attending seminars and symposia instead of at his hospital duties. Yes, he had spent two days a week at the main hospital, far too little in Dr Ingham's view. He himself would be taking a very different line.

He had been asked to take over as locum, then?

Of course. It was only a temporary measure. The health authority were bound as a matter of form to advertise the post, but, naturally, the senior registrar would normally be looked to.

Alec wondered if Dr Pritti's frank opinion of Ingham's chances could be biased, or whether Ingham was really too obtuse to see the situation or too afraid to admit it to himself. Certainly, his expectation of getting the post seemed to be genuine, and his smugness was distasteful. In fact, the general impression Ingham gave was that Swainson had been a mediocre consultant with an overblown reputation, who was well out of the way.

'Did you yourself get on well with him?' Alec asked.

'I did my best,' Ingham replied. 'It is important that senior colleagues should have an efficient working relationship. I must say, with Dr Swainson it was something of an uphill battle, but it was plainly my duty to try. I expect you realize, too, that he was rather inclined to play on his position as consultant to overawe the younger and more impressionable staff. Particularly female staff.'

'Are you telling me that Dr Swainson used his position to obtain sexual favours?' Alec asked sharply. Dr Ingham was the only one so far who had shown no reluctance to tarnish his colleague's name.

'I did not say that,' Ingham replied huffily. 'You are putting words into my mouth, Inspector, and you are not entitled to do that.'

'What are you saying, then?' Alec pressed, but Ingham withdrew evasively.

On the subject of his own movements over the weekend, Dr Ingham was more forthcoming. On Friday he had been on duty. Over the weekend Dr Swainson had been on call, so Ingham had the weekend free. He had done some gardening on Saturday, gone shopping with his wife, and on Sunday read the papers in the morning, taking the family to the coast later in the day. On Monday morning he had come into work as usual, to be met by the news that Dr Swainson had died and that he was to stand in as locum consultant for the time being.

'Do you know how Dr Swainson died?'

He was trapped in the mortuary, Dr Ingham had heard, and had frozen to death.

Alec looked at his notes and decided to call a halt. Somehow, he found Dr Ingham naturally antipathetic, and it took an effort to remind himself that he was looking for the true murderer of Geoffrey Swainson and not just for a plausible suspect. He took Dr Ingham's home address and left.

It took Alec half an hour to find the Inghams' house in a maze of similar properties on a new estate. It was newer, and larger, than he had expected somehow, but a senior registrar's salary, after several years in post, should not be ungenerous. Mrs Ingham came to the door in response to his ring and it was immediately plain that her husband had warned her by phone that Alec might call.

'If you're asking about Dr Swainson's death I know nothing about it, and nor does Roger.' She stood squarely in the doorway, arms folded, gripping her shoulders with her hands.

'If I could come in . . . ?' Alec inquired mildly.

'No, I'm afraid you can't. I don't want to answer any questions, and besides,' she added illogically, 'you haven't shown me anything to prove who you are.' Alec proffered his warrant card, which was ignored. 'I know nothing, and I've got a busy day today, and besides, I'm not feeling well. If you want to ask any questions you must do it when Roger's here, and besides, you can't do it unless we have a solicitor.'

She made as if to shut the door. Alec took a step forward so that she would literally have to shut it in his face and said politely, 'If you feel like that, Mrs Ingham, I won't ask you anything now, but I shall come back, with a policewoman, and I shall ask one or two things then. I'm bound to say that your manner is unhelpful and I would remind you that it is your duty as a citizen, and in law, to answer questions properly put to you by the police.'

As Alec had guessed, Mrs Ingham's bluster was easily quashed. He wondered whether to follow it up and push his way in there and then, but he knew it would be a mistake. By this afternoon the Inghams would certainly have put their heads together, but that had to be accepted. Without a WPC or at least some other witness to the conversation he would be on sticky ground and he had no doubt that the Inghams would not overlook any lapse in procedure. They were very hot on their rights, he perceived ruefully, and so far as the present encounter was concerned it was better to quit while he was in front.

Back at Ovenden, Alec considered the possibility of lunch in the canteen, rejected it reluctantly and sent Johnson up for a sandwich. Meanwhile, he glanced through the chart Johnson had prepared tracing the mortuary keys over the weekend. The conclusion was inescapable. There were only three keys – officially, at any rate. One was on the key-ring of the head porter, on a hook in his little office. It was still there, and nobody remembered it being taken out over the weekend. Johnson had spoken with the porters who had been on duty over the weekend, and it seemed that one or other of them had been in the porters' room most of the time. They had a television in there and, though they sometimes used one of the general staff common rooms when they weren't busy, last weekend they both stayed watching their own TV. Alec had the impression that a crate of beer might have been added to the accoutrements of the porters' room over Friday night, a good enough reason for not being more sociable.

The second key was held at the switchboard, and this was the one the undertakers' men had used on Monday morning when they went to remove the body of Florence Timms. Keys held at reception had to be signed out, and were also checked at the end of each receptionist's shift, though privately Alec thought that this was the kind of routine which was likely to be skimped from familiarity. However, Mary was sure that the keys had been on their rack when she took over at eight on Saturday morning, and no one had asked for them while she was on duty, which was up till three that afternoon.

The third key was kept by Miss Carmel. It remained with her, as chief administrator, in a key cupboard in her office. It had been there on Friday night, she said. On Monday, when she had come in first thing, it was missing. Miss Carmel had described the tag which identified it and there was no doubt that it was this key which had been found on the floor of the mortuary by the scene of crime team. Alec sighed and wished that Miss Carmel had volunteered this information when they had first spoken.

It looked as if Dr Swainson had certainly come into the hospital on Saturday morning, had used Miss Carmel's key to let himself into the mortuary, had, if the evidence of the tear in the table top could be believed, sat down and started to write the cremation form out, when . . . what? And what was it Dr Pritti had said about the cremation form itself going missing? Alec reached again for the phone.

'Miss Carmel? Sorry to trouble you. Florence Timms, the elderly woman who died last week. There's some difficulty about the cremation form, I hear?'

'There was. It's all cleared up now. They've taken the body away.'

'Did it turn up?'

'No. We had to do a duplicate. Of course, we have to be careful about that when a form goes missing because of the possibility of fraud, but the counterfoil's been amended and we let the coroner's office know just in case.'

'Quite so. Who was the junior doctor who attended Florence Timms?'

'Harriet Shepherd.'

'And she signed the form as well?'

'Yes, as the doctor who treated the patient and last attended her.'

'I wonder if I could have a word with Dr Shepherd?'

Miss Carmel hesitated, and her voice sounded puzzled. 'If you wish, of course. I'll have her bleeped and ask her to come over, shall I?'

'I'd be most grateful.' Alec hesitated, uncertain whether to mention the key, and decided against for the time being.

DC Johnson came in with the inevitable cup of coffee and a salad roll.

'Is WPC Simmonds still up there?' Alec asked. Johnson nodded. 'Nip back up and ask her to come over directly, if you would.'

Johnson was back with Jayne Simmonds in a very short time, and Alec waved her to a chair in the corner of his office.

'Thanks, Andy. Look, there'll be a Dr Shepherd along in a moment. Show her in, will you, and then I want you to check the whereabouts for the whole of Saturday and

72

Sunday of the following. Miss Carmel, Dr Norman, a Dr Ingham who's from the district general hospital, and this Dr Shepherd. Got that? That should keep you going for a while. Now, Jayne,' he continued as the door shut, 'I just want you to sit in while I talk to Dr Shepherd, then we've one or two more visits to make. Take notes, and I'll give you the nod if there's anything I want verbatim. OK?'

'Right, sir.' Jayne Simmonds settled in her chair and crossed her legs, wishing she had not had quite so many cups of coffee during her researches in the canteen.

Harriet Shepherd was a mousy girl with a defensive air which might be natural when summoned from her duties to speak to a policeman. She seemed to have little of the habit of authority common to doctors. No doubt that would grow, thought Alec; she could not long be out of medical school and a lack of confidence in herself was reflected in clothes that sat uneasily together, quenching any spark of sexual attractiveness. She took the chair Alec indicated and sat gracelessly chewing at a torn fingernail.

'Now, Dr Shepherd,' Alec began, 'thank you for coming to see me. I wanted just to clear up in my own mind a few points about the death of your patient, Florence Timms. I expect you know that Dr Swainson has been found dead in the mortuary.' He watched keenly for her reaction to this blunt announcement, but she merely nodded curtly and he continued, 'As the body of Florence Timms was there too we must naturally pursue one or two points. Now, you had completed a cremation form for Florence Timms, I understand. That would have to be countersigned by a more senior doctor?'

'By another doctor, yes,' said Dr Shepherd touchily.

'And that other doctor in this instance was Dr Swainson?'

'Yes.'

'And for that he would have to view the body,' Alec continued patiently.

'Yes.'

'Why?'

'To make sure it was the right one. And that the cause of death was as given on the form,' said Dr Shepherd, as to an idiot.

'How could he check these points? I mean, presumably he wouldn't know the patient?'

Dr Shepherd sighed rudely and seemed to resign herself to lengthy explanation. 'He'd identify the body from the label on the shroud. It'd still have the wrist tag on as well, if he wanted to be fussy. It's just a routine.'

'Yes,' Alec pursued, 'but the routine is designed to prevent mistakes. I mean, a label on a shroud is hardly foolproof identification.'

'What do you want? She could hardly tell him who she was herself.'

'And as to the cause of death? How could Dr Swainson check that was properly recorded? What was the cause of death, out of interest?'

'Bronchial pneumonia. Just bloody old age, really. It could have been anything, 'flu, whatever. It just happened to be pneumonia.'

Alec suppressed his instinctive dislike of women who swore and asked, 'Would Dr Swainson be able to confirm the diagnosis? Without a post-mortem, I mean.'

'Of course not. It's just a formality, I told you. The form has to be signed by two doctors.'

'It wasn't likely that Dr Swainson would query the cause of death? I mean, does that ever happen?'

'I doubt it. Not in this case, certainly. Why should he? Old people don't live forever.'

'Probably just as well. Perhaps we should have euthanasia at seventy anyway. It'd save a lot of trouble all round, don't you think?'

'Maybe we should. Only, I don't expect we'll see it that way when we're seventy ourselves.'

'It's a bit of a puzzle what happened to the crem form, isn't it?' Alec said. 'Didn't it get mislaid and you had to fill in a new one?'

'Yes. Bloody nuisance. The relatives had to delay the funeral and they didn't like that much. Of course, it was me that got the brunt of their moans.'

'Who signed the second form, apart from yourself?'

'Pete Haines. Obstetric registrar.'

'Do you think, Dr Shepherd, that that first form might have been taken to conceal something? Was it that Dr Swainson didn't agree with the diagnosis? Or was it that Florence Timms's end was helped along a little? Did he decide he didn't want to sign that form after all? You wouldn't want a thing like that to become known, would you, Dr Shepherd? Let me suggest something. You stole that form, Dr Shepherd. You stole it to destroy it, so no one would ever know.'

'I never did.' The girl started out of her seat, her grammar slipping as her temper rose. 'What the hell do you mean? You mean I killed Swainson as well, because there'd be no point in stealing the form if he was alive to tell everyone about it? Well, I didn't. I didn't! There was nothing wrong with the bloody form, it was what I said, she died of pneumonia, you're just trying to find someone you can pin the bloody murder on, aren't you? You're all the same, fucking pigs.' Dr Shepherd's thin professional skin crumpled altogether as she slumped in her chair, crying uglily. Alec watched her in silence, while Jayne Simmonds's pencil scratched to a halt.

Alec got up and opened the door, then walked past the weeping Dr Shepherd to stand staring out of the window.

'Jayne, show Dr Shepherd where she can wash her face. That's all for now, Dr Shepherd. Thank you.'

He gazed out of the window while Jayne Simmonds led the snuffling Dr Shepherd gently out of the room, and thought how Diana would despise his behaviour. He had learnt something worthwhile; at least he thought he had. The cost had been the stripping of Dr Shepherd's dignity, and the hatred of the police that she would carry for the rest of her life; and probably the destruction of an already fragile self-respect.

'I've left her to it,' Jayne Simmonds said quietly. Alec turned to thank her, but she avoided his eyes.

'Did you really think there was something wrong with the old woman's death, sir?'

'It was a possibility,' Alex replied. 'I thought it had to be checked out, but for what it's worth, I think Dr Swainson had already signed the form, or was in the process of doing so, when whatever it was happened as a result of which he ended up in the fridge.'

'You think he was killed in the mortuary itself?'

'Well, strictly he wasn't killed, since we know he was alive when he went into the drawer. He was rendered unconscious somehow, and yes, I think that was done in the mortuary itself, though I'm blowed if I know how. Maybe a drug, as we're in a hospital, though that doesn't explain how it was given to him without him noticing.'

'I asked everyone in the canteen, sir, without being too pushy, about Dr Swainson. Everybody agreed that he didn't get on too well with his wife – the women, that is. None of the men I spoke to had noticed one way or the other, but then men never do.'

'Quite,' said Alec drily. 'And what was the consensus about his current affair?'

'Nobody knew,' said Jayne. 'It seemed to be common knowledge that he'd been involved with a junior doctor until she moved on some months ago. General opinion was that if there hasn't been one since, then it won't be long coming.'

That tallied with Mary's observations, even if it got them no further. 'OK, well, we'd better have another word with Dr Norman. Like to give her a ring and tell her we'll be calling? Then she can't make a song and dance when we turn up. Don't let her put you off, though, she'll walk all over you if you let her. Make it later in the afternoon.' Alec looked at his watch. 'We've a call to make on Mrs Ingham first.'

Jayne nodded and went out.

When Alec and WPC Simmonds reached the Inghams' house, it was to find a car in the drive and the door opened by Dr Ingham in aggressive mood.

'My wife says you came round here and tried to force your way in this morning,' he began, before Alec had time to greet him. 'I've rung my solicitor and he says you were acting outside your authority and we have a good case for complaint.'

'Good afternoon, Dr Ingham,' said Alec cheerfully. 'Your wife will recall, I'm sure, that we spoke only on the doorstep, and that when she was reluctant to answer my few brief inquiries I immediately accepted the situation and arranged to call back this afternoon with a woman police officer. Now, here I am, and this is WPC Simmonds, and I should be grateful if I could have a few words with Mrs Ingham. May we come in?'

'I think I ought to ring my solicitor again. You can't ask my wife anything she doesn't want to answer. I know my rights.'

I wish you did, Alec thought, then we could get on with things. Knowing the trip had been a waste of time, he went on, 'By all means ring your solicitor. By all means ask him to be present. But I should still like to speak to

Mrs Ingham. What is your reason for refusing to let me do so?'

'I didn't say I was refusing,' said Dr Ingham truculently.

'Good. Then we'll come in.'

The doctor hesitated, then grudgingly held the door open for them. They went through into a living-room which was strangely spartan for such a house. Alec wondered whether he had underestimated the Inghams' good taste, then realized that what he was looking at was the effect of shortness of cash. The house was detached, the district new but good. Had Dr Ingham been pushing the boat out further than was wise?

Alec's purpose in visiting Mrs Ingham had been to collect her version of her husband's movements over the weekend, to see if there was any discrepancy in their accounts which might cover a trip to Ovenden. That there was no love lost between Ingham and his consultant, and that Ingham stood to gain from Swainson's death seemed plain, but now that he had seen the inside of the house, Alec was inclined to think that Ingham's need for promotion might be more pressing than he had first thought. However, interviewing Mrs Ingham with her husband present would be a waste of time, and so it proved.

Yes, she had been with her husband all weekend, either at home or out shopping. Where had they done their shopping? Actually, they had rather combed the area, since they were looking for some tiles for the bathroom, so they had been to several places as well as their weekly trip to the supermarket. All local? No, some further away; and when pressed, Mrs Ingham listed them, including a DIY centre about six miles the far side of Ovenden. And this was Saturday afternoon? Well, it was about one when they went, after an early lunch, getting back at half past three or so. And the morning they had spend round the house? Yes, hadn't they said so? And on Sunday? On Sunday they had gone to the coast. What was this, questioning them as if they were suspects? Surely that was outside his authority, a violation of their rights as innocent citizens. Dr Ingham was going to get his solicitor to complain to Alec's superiors about his attitude and was sure they would have something to say to him. No doubt Alec was new to the job and when he had a little more experience he would realize that he could not browbeat people in this way. Considering Alec's youth and his own position Dr Ingham was inclined to think it an impertinence. Alec sighed and they left.

'If he didn't say so much, I'd be more inclined to cross him off the list,' Alec said as they drove away. 'Can you really believe that a man like that is capable of an intelligent murder? A stupid one, yes. Still, he protests too much. On the list he'll have to stay. What's the time?'

It was just on four. 'Fancy a cuppa and a cream scone?' Alec asked with a sideways glance.

'Yes,' Jayne said, surprised, 'that would be nice.'

'Good. There's a place along here somewhere, I remember. Just have to hope the Super doesn't come past and see the car.'

They sat in the shade of a fruit tree in the little tea-garden at the rear of the café while the waitress brought a pot of tea and the scones. Alec watched Jayne Simmonds bite into her scone with youthful zest, and caught her eye. She grinned, licking cream from round her mouth.

'I've always enjoyed cream teas,' she confessed. 'It's the only chance you get as an adult to get really sticky like a kid. I suppose there might be a ladylike way of eating cream scones, but I don't know it, I'm afraid.'

'You go right ahead,' Alec smiled. 'May as well get value for money.'

He sat back and reviewed the case in his mind. Swainson had been discovered yesterday morning, so no one could say Alec had wasted much time, even if he was a long way from a conclusion. The picture was beginning to build up in his mind, of Swainson at the centre of a web of relationships. One of those relationships had given rise to murder. How it had been done might become clear, or it might not, but Alec was confident that he would find the 'who' and the 'why'. The 'how' could follow on. The trouble was, in a place like a hospital so many people had the means and the know-how to achieve death, and a surprising number seemed to have had the motive as well. He began to wish Dr Swainson had been considerate enough to be murdered at home, where the list of suspects could be kept within sensible bounds. There could be all sorts of possibilities which he had not even considered, people with a grudge against Dr Swainson who knew, or chanced on the fact, that he would be in the mortuary that Saturday morning.

He became aware that Jayne was speaking.

'I was saying, don't let your tea get cold,' she said, smiling and he thought what an attractive picture she made, sitting in the white-painted wrought-iron chair, neat in a pleated skirt and cream blouse, her suede jacket hung over the back of the chair, swinging her leg a little.

'Time we were going,' Alec said hastily, and drained his cup. 'We've Dr Norman to see, and I'm not looking forward to it very much. I've some questions to put to her that she'll find distinctly offensive and I fancy she'll be on the phone to some of her chums in Whitehall Palace before we're even out of the door. Ready?'

Jayne gathered up her bag and jacket. 'Ready. And thank you, sir, that was really nice.'

* * *

This time they all three avoided the deep armchairs, sitting instead round a polished dining table. Jayne Simmonds unobtrusively picked a notebook out of her bag and settled it in her lap. Alec leant forward.

'Dr Norman,' he began, 'you run a clinic in family planning, and one in venereology.'

Angela Norman nodded.

'So you are used to dealing with these matters sensibly and dispassionately. Last time we called, I asked you a question about possible affairs you or your husband might have had, and you took offence. Now, I am going to ask you some more questions about your relationship with your husband. Your sexual relationship.' She pursed her lips. 'I want you to answer these questions quite clinically and factually. I assure you that they are relevant to the inquiry, or I should not trouble you with them. I assure you too that I am quite as used to discussing these matters on an objective basis as you are, so neither of us need feel embarrassed or prudish.' Which isn't quite true, Alec thought, but it'll have to do.

'Did you enjoy a normal sexual relationship with your husband?'

'Of course.' Dr Norman sat impassively and Alec, who had thought she would refuse to answer, relaxed a fraction.

'But you never had children. Was that through choice?'

'Not entirely. We tried to have children, earlier in our careers, but perhaps we didn't try very hard. Later, it would have been less appropriate, and we stopped trying.'

'While continuing to enjoy a normal sexual relationship in other respects?'

She nodded.

'Quite. Do you know the reason you were unable to have a child? Was one of you infertile?'

81

'I really don't see . . . no, I don't know the reason. As I say, we didn't try very hard and then the moment passed, we were both very busy.'

'So you didn't try to find out why?'

'No.'

Alec let that one go. Perhaps her interest in family planning came later; nevertheless, it seemed a curious admission. He took a deep breath.

'Dr Norman, you do know that your husband had had affairs?'

Yes, this time she admitted it quietly, she did know there had been occasions, in the past. Away on conferences, and so forth. Not many men were totally faithful in such circumstances.

And more serious affairs?

There might have been.

Did she in fact know of any of the women concerned?

Not at the time. In due course, hospital gossip had filtered back to her.

Dr Swainson never openly acknowledged his unfaithfulness?

No.

Were there indications that an affair was currently in progress?

Dr Norman hesitated. 'I couldn't be sure, Inspector, and indeed I preferred not to speculate in that way. As you say, I knew that there was a possibility that Geoffrey was unfaithful. I found that pretty hard to take, and I suppose like anyone else in that situation I tried to shut my mind to it, pretend it wasn't happening. If you tell me that he had someone at the moment, I suppose I couldn't really say I was surprised.'

'But you've no idea who it might be. No hospital rumours in this case? It would be likely to be somebody at the hospital?'

'That would be consistent. As for who it was, no, I don't know, unless . . . '

'Yes?'

'It's only that . . . I noticed he was rather casual recently when he talked about Jo – you know how people play a little game when there's someone they're really interested in, of being elaborately careless about them. But Geoffrey was always rather casual about people anyway, so I'm probably mistaken.'

'Jo – that would be the secretary, Miss Carmel?'

'I . . . it's awkward, isn't it? I may be perfectly mistaken. It seems awful to cast aspersions on someone. Especially someone you like. We know her fairly well.'

Did Dr Swainson's wanderings diminish, or take away, their own sexual relations?

A hesitation. To some extent, was the eventual reply.

Did he have any particular fads, sexually? Anything he found especially titillating? Alec kept his voice neutral.

Not especially. Like most couples, they had explored the normal repertoire of sexual behaviour. Dr Norman's expression was cool.

Within the last week, things had stayed normal, there had been no difference in Dr Swainson's attitude towards his wife, or hers to him?

None.

And they had had intercourse . . . how often?

The chill deepened. 'Three times.'

'The last time being when?'

'Friday night. I don't know . . . '

'Normal straightforward intercourse?'

Angela Norman's anger finally overflowed. How dare he pretend that questions like these had any bearing on Geoffrey's death? It was just an excuse for him to enjoy a voyeurist's pleasure, like looking through dirty magazines. No doubt it gave him something to masturbate over later. Jayne Simmonds reddened and stared at her notebook. Alec hoped she would not forget to write in it also.

'Was it normal straightforward intercourse?'

'How dare you! I'm going to –'

'Was it?'

'You dirty-minded –'

'Was it normal straightforward intercourse?'

'Yes, damn you, yes!'

'Thank you. You've been very patient,' Alec said sweetly, 'and now we'll leave you in peace.'

Dr Norman faltered. She's going to change her mind, Alec thought; she's going to say perhaps she'd forgotten. Friday? Oh yes, Friday they'd done other things instead. But she collected herself and shut her mouth angrily. Alec rose, with a glance to Jayne, and led the way out.

'I certainly shall complain this time,' Angela Norman said as they stood on the doorstep. 'I should have done last time. You'll be taken off this case, Inspector Stainton. It's disgraceful that my husband should be treated this way after he's dead.'

'It's because he's dead,' Alec said, 'that it happens. Goodbye.'

As they walked away down the gravel to the car parked in the roadway, Jayne said, 'Would you tell me why that was necessary, sir? I'd just like to know.'

Alec looked down at her. 'Only that we suspected that Dr Swainson hadn't slept with his wife for some time. And we know that he didn't sleep with anyone on Friday night – not in the normal way. He might have had oral sex, so I had to press the point.'

'Do you think she just didn't want to talk about it with us? I mean, maybe they did have that on Friday and she was shy of saying so.'

'She's a specialist in that sort of thing. Professionally, I mean. Hardly likely to be shy about talking about it.'

'Still, it's a bit different when it's yourself, sir, isn't it?'

'Mm. She was guessing, Jayne. When I asked her when they last had intercourse she had to guess whether to say Friday. She guessed we might be able to tell whether Swainson had had it or not, and knowing her husband she guessed he had – only not with her. He wasn't here on Friday night at all. And if he wasn't at home, where was he?'

'Presumably he was with a lover,' said the ACC later on the telephone.

'Yes. Or just possibly she was,' said Alec. 'Either way, her evidence about his movements on Saturday morning disappears into thin air. It probably also lets her off the list of suspects for the time being.'

'Hm. I quite see why you had to pursue the matter, though I don't really understand why she should choose to lie about it. However, there's no doubt it's caused quite a stink. It's as well, perhaps, that you did prove she was lying, otherwise your behaviour would be hard to justify. What's your next move?'

Alec glanced up at the clock, which said a quarter to eight. 'Obviously, we want to know why Dr Norman wasn't telling the truth. More important, if Swainson wasn't at home, where he was, and who last saw him alive. So far, we've got no further than Friday afternoon, when several people spoke to him. Do you think we could have a look round the house?'

'Ask her – no, I'll ask her. If she agrees, fine, but if she doesn't I don't think we really have enough to force the issue. I'll speak to her now and ring you back. You'll still be there?'

'I will. Till you call, anyway, sir.'

'Good lad. I'll be as quick as I can, then if you're able I should nip off home if I were you. I'm a great believer in being fresh in the morning rather than stale in the evening.'

'Thank you, sir. I've got my report to do for the Superintendent, then I'll take your advice.'

'Hr'm, yes, the Superintendent. Well, I shouldn't make a great point of coming here personally to give it to him, if I were you. This complaint from Dr Norman has rather got under his skin, though I shouldn't really be telling you that.'

The ACC rang off and Alec turned to the report, picking it out on the typewriter with three fingers. Johnson and WPC Simmonds had been sent home half an hour ago with instructions to be bright and early in the morning.

He was laboriously working his way through the final paragraph when the telephone rang again.

'Sorry,' the ACC said. 'No reply on the phone, so we had a local car call. Seems she's gone out: house locked and car gone. I think we'll leave that one while we see what else you come up with.'

'Right, sir, I'll work at it from another angle and see where I get to.'

'Very well. Keep me in touch. Good night.'

Alec was put out to find that Diana had a visitor when he got home, but the delight on her face at seeing him seemed genuine, and he told himself it was mere selfishness to expect her to languish on her own in his absence. The visitor, a man of Alec's age or a little more, sized up the situation in a moment and began to make his apologies: must dash, glad to have met Alec, Diana had talked about him a lot.

'Who was that?' Alec asked as the door shut behind him.

'Jem. Friend from college. He's got a fellowship now. He rang to tell me and I asked him over. It's nice to have you back. I thought I wasn't going to see you for a couple of weeks.'

She hugged him warmly and Alec realized how tense the day had made him. He sat contentedly with a glass of sherry, gazing out of the big bay window while Diana bustled around getting a meal together and asking him questions through the half-open door.

'So the beastly Superintendent has been overruled? You realize he'll only try and take it out on you some other way?'

'Mm. But at least I've been given the chance, and it shows people are taking an interest in how I'm doing.'

'And you really think you can solve it? It'd be impressive to have a successful murder case to your credit, wouldn't it. Who do you think did it?'

'Ask me another. It's usually someone close to the victim, but that seems to cover everyone or no one in this case, depending on how you look at it.'

'What d'you mean?'

'Only that there were plenty of people close to him in one sense, but no one seems to have really known him.'

'What about his wife?'

'She ought to be suspect number one at the moment, but we haven't really got a case against her. We're at a very early stage yet.'

'Does she have an alibi?'

Alec sighed. 'We're still checking things like that. It all takes so long. You think you're getting on so well, dashing around and so on, then when you look back at the day you find hardly anything's been achieved.'

'Seems to me you need more people on the job. Then

you could set them all the routine things while you sit smoking your meerschaum pipe engaged in brilliant deduction.' Diana came through from the kitchen and set a plate and mat down on the table beside Alec. He smelt the delightful odour of grilled mushrooms and realized how hungry he was.

'I think we do need more people,' he answered, picking up the knife and fork, 'it's just that there aren't that many available at the moment. Anyway, throwing numbers at a problem isn't always the way to solve it. I do love you.'

'Ah, that's satisfied hunger talking. What you love is having someone to welcome you home and cook you a meal. That is not quite the same thing, wouldn't you agree?'

'Uh-uh.' Alec shook his head and swallowed a mouthful of bacon. 'I accept your reasoning but deny your conclusion. As I shall demonstrate later, if I have the energy.'

When they lay contentedly in bed, Diana said, 'Does it worry you, that you're dealing with someone's death? I mean, that one of the people you're interviewing has presumably killed another human being?'

Alec thought. 'No. You don't think of it like that. It's more of a problem in the abstract that has to be solved, at the same time as other people are doing their best to hide the clues. I'm . . . I suppose I do wish, sometimes, that murder wasn't so . . . uncivilized. It does taint everything around it, everyone who comes into contact with it, to some degree.'

'You mean, you too?' Diana asked gently.

'Yes.'

Diana rolled on her side so that she could look at him. After a while, she said quietly, 'That's the other side, isn't it? Not the glamour and the boost to your career, but what it does to you on the way. What you have to do to yourself.'

'Yes.'

'Alec, I can't help you there.'

'Just be here, to remind me of the other side, the ordinary side.'

'I'll try,' she said doubtfully.

Comforted, Alec slept. But it was a long while before Diana could compose her own mind sufficiently to sleep.

Chapter Six

Johnson had been despatched to county HQ with the previous day's report; WPC Simmonds pottered about making the inevitable cup of coffee. Alec glanced at his watch and dialled the secretary's number on the internal exchange.

Miss Carmel was cool when she heard what Alec was after. Personal files were personal files, she said, and were not for disclosure. Medical records even less so.

Alec reminded her of the gravity of the investigation and suggested that they would certainly have to be disclosed when the matter came to court, and that if need be he would apply directly to the courts now for an order for disclosure. Miss Carmel prevaricated, replying that perhaps that might be the best way of proceeding, knowing as well as he the sort of delays which would be involved. Eventually they compromised. Personal records, which listed previous employments, references and so forth, would be made available. Medical records, Miss Carmel regretted, must be regarded as absolutely confidential and would not be released. Alec thanked her and, as an afterthought, asked if she would mind bringing the files over personally. They arranged a time later in the morning and Alec rang off. Without replacing the receiver, he dialled the switchboard and asked for an outside line.

'Nip over to the switchboard at reception,' he said to Jayne, cupping his hand over the mouthpiece. 'Maybe I'm over-suspicious, but I'd rather this call wasn't overheard. Engage the girl in conversation or something if she seems inclined to listen in. Do it without upsetting her.'

A moment later, Alec was speaking to the police doctor, arranging for him to try an informal approach which might lead to some information on Dr Swainson's medical history.

'Incidentally, Peter,' he added, 'I hope you meant it when you said Swainson hadn't had intercourse for a day or two.'

'Did I say that? Yes, well, I should certainly be very surprised if he had.'

'Don't back off now, for heaven's sake. It actually could be quite significant for where he spent the night.'

'Um. Let's say that we'd be prepared to back it in court, but we couldn't undertake to prove it to the satisfaction of a sceptical judge.'

'Thanks a lot. I may have just committed professional hara kiri in the naïve belief that what you said was gospel.'

'Sorry about that,' Peter said easily. 'Anything else I can help with?'

'No, that's fine. Do your best on the records, won't you?'

Alec put the phone down and sat back, sipping thoughtfully at his coffee. Jayne Simmonds returned and he set her to tracking down the women Mary had referred to as having had affairs with Swainson.

'I think it might be profitable to have a discreet word with each of them. If they've scattered to the four corners of the earth we'll have to get their local force to send someone to have a chat, otherwise I'd like to talk to them myself if I can. OK?'

'Right, sir.'

'Good girl.'

* * *

Alec settled back and reached for Johnson's notes on the Saturday alibis.

Johnson had started with Dr Ingham who by his own admission had been shopping with his wife, not far from Ovenden, in the early afternoon. Johnson had checked with the DIY store, a large warehouse type unit on a trading estate, and found that till receipts were coded according to the general category of the goods bought. He had then on his own initiative rung Mrs Ingham and obtained from her, with many complaints, a list of the items they had bought. He then rang back to the manager and asked him to search the computer record to match this list with the till receipt, using the individual price code for each item. Sure enough, the records showed that just such a list of items had been purchased, and also gave the till number. The manager helpfully offered to ask the till girl whether she remembered anything of the purchasers, only to ring back later to say that the girl had, unsurprisingly, no way of lifting the purchasers of these items from the hundreds she had served on Saturday.

Alec heard Johnson come into the other room and looked through to find him just sitting down at his desk.

'Just pop in, will you, Andy? I'm running through these alibis.'

Johnson came through, obviously gratified to be consulted. Alec remembered that he had been using Jayne for the most interesting tasks so far, and wondered whether Johnson were resentful. Jayne Simmonds was, after all, uniformed branch while Johnson was CID.

'This alibi of Ingham's. You've done very well, chasing it up. Anything which isn't down here, which you came across? Any impressions?'

'Not really, sir.' Johnson looked as if he would like to be able to come up with something very much indeed. 'I mean, you noticed the time, sir.'

Alec swore, and looked again at the details of the till receipt which Johnson had taken down over the phone. There was the date – and the time: 11.24. And Ingham had said they were out from one till three-thirty or so. Allowing for natural error, they must still have left the house at eleven at the latest, even if they had gone to the DIY store first, and not last as Ingham had implied. Alec looked at the details again, to see what else he had missed.

'Did the manager tell you what all these codes represent? Yes, you've written it down underneath.'

Alec skimmed through the list. Screws. Adhesive. A tile cutter. That supported part of Dr Ingham's account, anyway, even if no tiles had been bought.

'Nothing very substantial, is there?' Alec mused.

'Sir?'

'I mean, I know shopping is supposed to be a leisure activity these days, but would you really drive out to a place like this merely to buy half a dozen small items you could get as easily in the hardware shop round the corner?'

'They probably thought they could get the tiles there, too, then didn't like the choice.'

'Probably. Just suppose, though, that you wanted to provide yourself with an alibi. All these items are quite small. I mean, you could leave someone there to do the shopping and come back for them quite a bit later, provided they didn't have anything awkward or heavy to deal with. Or they could go home by bus. Meanwhile you – or Ingham – take the car another six miles to keep an appointment with Dr Swainson. Possible?'

'Possible, sir, but if you've got an alibi you've gone to such trouble over, why lie about when you went out? I mean, surely Ingham'd have drawn our attention to the alibi himself, not told a fib about going in the afternoon instead.'

'Mm. Still, I fancy Dr Ingham moves a step up the suspect list. See if you can get a line later on his financial condition. I mean, if he was really desperate for money, the temptation to procure his own promotion could be just too much.'

Alec looked on down the list. The next name was that of Miss Carmel, who had told Johnson that she had slept in on Saturday morning, as was her habit.

'I did ask if she lived alone, sir. She rather bit my head off for that. Anyway, there's no one else registered at her address on the electoral roll, so there shouldn't be anyone long term.'

Miss Carmel had taken her time about getting up, had a leisurely breakfast cum lunch, and spent the afternoon in the garden.

'No shopping?' Alec asked.

'Says she always does it on a Friday night, when they stay open late, to save the crush. She gave me the impression of being a very organized lady, sir.'

'But it was her key we found in the mortuary. Hm. Well, she obviously had the opportunity to get rid of Swainson, though you might expect her to rig up some sort of alibi. So she stays on the list. Who's next?'

'Dr Shepherd, sir. She wasn't terribly helpful, so I've had to guess a bit at her movements, but there's a certain amount of corroboration by nurses and so on.'

'Does Dr Shepherd wear high heels?'

'Sir?'

'Never mind. Thinking aloud. So she was on duty on the geriatric wards all day?'

'There are several spells when we don't know exactly where she was, as you see, sir. Any one of those would be long enough for her to nip over to the mortuary.'

'Mm. Motive? I suppose she could be the mystery woman with whom Swainson spent the night – but then, so could any of a hundred women. That missing cremation form still nags me. Someone obviously couldn't let it be found, but for what reason?'

'Do you think there was something dodgy about it, sir?'

'If it's not the form itself, then there's something about it which shows how or when Swainson was stuck in the drawer, and by whom. Anyway, so far as motive for Shepherd is concerned, we've got possible funny business over that form, or she was Swainson's mystery lover. Neither seems very likely, but she clearly had opportunity so we'll leave her in. Now, you've added Mary to the list.'

'Yes, sir. After all, she had easy access to one set of keys. On the face of it she seems an unlikely suspect, but I thought that ought not to sway us.'

'Just so. But from your notes here, it seems she was tied to the switchboard just about all morning on Saturday. At any rate, she couldn't have anticipated when she might have a free moment, so if she did it, she was an opportunist. She had a coffee-break. Yes, I see, all accounted for.'

'Definitely seen in the canteen, sir.'

'Good. Mary stays on the list, but at the bottom. I'm glad. She's too good a witness to be guilty herself. That leaves . . . ?'

'Dr Norman, sir. And she's accounted for all day.'

'Plenty of motive, with jealousy of Swainson's lovers – though why she should get homicidal now, when it's been going on so long, would be a mystery. Let's just say she came to the boil on Saturday. Or perhaps this man friend of hers comes into the picture. Say she wanted to marry him, or Swainson was being unreasonable, or . . . plenty of motive, then, but precious little opportunity, from what you've put down here.'

'That's right. She ran her clinic from ten till one, and I've got a list of her appointments.'

'Did they all turn up?'

'Two gaps. Eleven-twenty and eleven-fifty-five. There's a receptionist there, though, a nurse who sorts the patients out, and she reckons Dr Norman didn't leave the building all morning. She thinks Dr Norman took a call at eleven-twenty, she heard the phone, and at eleven-fifty-five she took her a cup of tea.'

'There is another way out if she did want to slip away?'

'Yes, sir.'

There was a knock at the door, and Alec looked at his watch.

'That'll be Miss Carmel,' he said.

Josephine Carmel looked cool and efficient in a pastel shirt-waister, and she bore a pile of buff files which she placed on a corner of Alec's desk.

'I'm trusting you rather beyond my own judgement in letting you have these,' she said. 'I must ask you to return them to me at the end of the day, and not to leave them unattended. Needless to say, the contents are confidential and are not for general transmission.'

She looked at him severely, one hand still on the files as if reluctant to relinquish her charge. Alec smiled reassuringly and gestured to the vacant chair. She took it with a reluctant smile and crossed her legs elegantly. Alec noted that she was wearing sandals with a low heel.

'I'd like to say that we are almost done and could leave you in peace shortly, but I'm afraid that wouldn't be very honest of me. To tell the truth, we don't know for certain how Dr Swainson came to be in the mortuary drawer, though it hardly seems that it could have been an accident.'

Miss Carmel frowned. 'I wish you could tell me something different. The more I think of someone deliberately putting him there, the less believable it all is. And what possible reason could there be for doing it?'

'There might be several,' Alec said carefully. 'Dr Swainson, like most people, had those who disliked or resented him. It is a question of degree, don't you think? You or I might talk against someone, but we should surely stop short of regarding that as justification for bringing about that person's death.'

'Of course. I should think anyone would.'

'Not everyone, Miss Carmel, or there would be no murders at all. In fact, in Dr Swainson's case there are possible reasons for a rather stronger resentment. You mentioned rumours about emotional relationships. Those rumours have some foundation.' He looked at her, and said gently, 'You knew that, didn't you?'

'Yes,' Miss Carmel said calmly.

'And you knew the people involved. The last one, for instance, was with a junior doctor, wasn't it? Who's now moved on?'

'Yes. I didn't see it as my business to pass on what I knew in confidence.'

'I said that was the last affair. That isn't strictly true, is it? There was another which was still going on up to Dr Swainson's death?'

Miss Carmel hesitated, one foot jigging slightly in its sandal.

'Do you know who that affair was with?'

She looked up. 'No.'

'So you don't know where Dr Swainson spent Friday night?'

'No.' There was a note of surprise in the secretary's voice.

'You see, Miss Carmel, when we know where Dr Swainson was on Friday night we can get a lot closer to finding out what happened on Saturday morning.'

'The inference being that he was with a lover. This lover would be your prime suspect, wouldn't she, Inspector?'

'Not necessarily. In fact, finding out who she may be would quite probably enable us to put her in the clear. So if you did know who it was, you might be doing her a favour by telling us.' Alec looked Miss Carmel in the eye. She held his gaze. 'If you should happen to find out . . . ?'

'I'll tell you, Inspector, yes,' she replied quietly. 'Now, I really – '

'Of course. Thanks for the files.' Alec leafed quickly through them. 'But I think you've overlooked one.'

Miss Carmel coloured. 'I don't think so.'

'Your own, Miss Carmel? Very natural to forget it. I'll send DC Johnson across with you and he can bring it back for me.' Alec rose with a polite smile. Miss Carmel hesitated, then stood up, smoothing her dress down. With a brief smile she turned and opened the door. Even then, Alec thought, she was on the brink of telling him something, then she drew herself up and abruptly, with small, quick steps, walked out. He watched her go, feeling that at last he was touching on the centre of the mystery.

'Nip over with Miss Carmel,' he said quickly to Johnson. 'She's got a file for you to bring back – it's her own personal file. Don't let her sort through it first. Though if she was going to, she's probably already done so.' Johnson followed Miss Carmel, and Alec returned to his desk, grinning.

Jayne Simmonds put her head round the door.

'Kettle's just boiled, sir. Like a cup?'

'Thanks. How're you getting along with the girlfriends?'

'Barely started yet, sir. Mary gave me the names so I went across to get some more details from the secretary, but she'd already left to come over here. Anyway, it looks as if we should track them down all right.'

'Good. Just out of interest, don't forget to check whether any of them happened to be over at Ovenden on Saturday. Or whether Swainson was still seeing any of them. Maybe that's where he was on Friday night.'

'Do you think so, sir?'

Alec smiled. 'Actually, no. I think we've a pretty good idea who Friday's date was with. With a bit of luck we'll get an admission before the day's out.'

Settling at his desk, Alec pulled the pile of files towards him. The day was warm, and through the open window came the sound of birdsong and the drone of insects. Voices carried across the grass from open windows in neighbouring buildings, snatches of television and the clatter of dishes, a testy exclamation. Suddenly, among the snatches of sound, Alec heard a voice he recognized and realized with a start that this was one of Dr Ingham's days at Ovenden in his new role as locum consultant. Unaccountably, Alec felt sorry for the man, as he heard the truculent voice briefly raised in argument. Awkward and a liar Ingham might be, but might not Alec himself be much the same if, at forty, he found his hopes and aspirations quenched, knowing himself to be stuck forever at his present level, and in financial straits caused by the discrepancy between ambition and reality? Even the temporary glory of being locum consultant must mock him with the knowledge that it could be snatched away as suddenly as it had come. Momentarily, Alec felt guilty at his own good fortune; the job he enjoyed, the prospect of advancement, Diana, the flat. Perhaps at this age Ingham too had been optimistic and contented, on track to a successful and secure future. Before his wife fell ill, before time slipped away and the other contestants in the race drew ahead, out of reach.

Dr Ingham's file was not in the pile since it was held at the district general hospital, so the first to hand was Dr Norman's. Alec opened the cover and began to read.

The contents of the file were in the main routine, the notes of salary increments, promotions and regradings, annual leave and sick leave, which make up the official record of a life. Alec traced in the yellowing papers Dr Norman's original appointment at Ovenden as a senior house officer, her marriage, after which she had taken her husband's name, quickly followed by a two-year break from her career. Alec imagined her in those two years whiling away her time in the big Victorian house in domestic chores and the housewife's daily round, waiting at first eagerly, then with less and less hope for pregnancy. After two years she returned to work and to her maiden name, no doubt to avoid confusion at Ovenden, starting her family planning clinic within a year and following a course of steadily increasing responsibility and status. Had that two-year absence been at the root of her interest in family planning matters? Had it also, perhaps, accounted for Dr Swainson's intrigues, as he became less willing to indulge a wife who saw making love only as a means of getting pregnant, and turned to less demanding partners? These were matters that the personal file, for all its name, gave no hint of.

Right at the back, faded papers recorded Dr Norman's arrival for interview from a junior post in another town, and there was a curriculum vitae and references. The CV hinted at another, youthful, Angela Norman who had been a prefect and a Queen's Guide, who played the cello well enough to give solo recitals at medical school concerts. The references were good, rather than glowing, giving a picture of a moderately talented student who worked hard to achieve good grades and applied herself diligently to her first hospital jobs. Noting the medical school, Alec speculated briefly about the old friend Mary had mentioned, the mysterious man who called for Dr Norman from time to time.

Alec pushed the file to one side and finished the coffee. It was cold, of course. The next file – they were in alphabetical order, naturally, since they had come from Miss Carmel – was that of Dr Shepherd, a thinner, newer file, barely dog-eared.

Harriet Shepherd had trained at the university thirty miles away which Alec just remembered in its earlier life as a polytechnic. Her father was a clerk with the Inland Revenue: nepotism was unlikely to have influenced Dr Shepherd's career. Alec read through the notes about her student days. The trend to continuous assessment meant far more of her teachers' judgements had been committed to paper than in the case of Angela Norman, who had qualified in the days of tutors who preferred 'a quiet word in your ear'. Alec noted a date and turned back a sheet to check. Yes, Harriet Shepherd had dropped a year at medical school, coming out a year later than those she had started with. He leafed through the papers until he came to the reason in a failed surgery exam. It was no surprise to find that Dr Shepherd was not a star pupil. Did this account for the chip on her shoulder, so conspicuous when Alec had talked to her? Other papers on the file bore witness to an academic career which teetered on the edge of being not quite good enough. Alec wondered whether the clerk father had eased the disappointment for his daughter, or merely turned the knife with his ambitions for her.

There were notes too of involvement in student activities referred to as 'an interest in topical and political issues' in the CV, but more bluntly as 'flirting with the hard left' in the comments of her tutor. There had been ill-advised demonstrations and expressions of solidarity, Alec noted, of the sort which would not be looked on favourably by the medical establishment. Altogether, it was a sorry and rather pathetic record, out of character so far as the popular conception of medical student life was concerned, but perhaps not so rare now with the far larger numbers entering medical school. Nothing, however, hinted at a tendency to get romantically involved with consultants, and certainly nothing suggested a reason for murder. Dr Shepherd seemed to be just as she appeared in the flesh: a more or less adequate doctor with an unengaging manner and a tendency to be her own worst enemy.

Alec glanced at his watch. It was lunch-time. Johnson had popped in to leave Miss Carmel's file on the desk and now Alec heard him go out to the canteen, chaffing WPC Simmonds.

The next file was that of Dr Swainson himself, and might have been the model for that of a successful and competent hospital doctor. From the respectable record as a student at a London teaching hospital, the file ranged over early hospital jobs, a smooth rise in rank, the first published research, shortly followed by a post as senior registrar, then consultant. Alec traced in the leave records the conferences, symposia and committees of a specialist who is well regarded and in strong demand. No black marks, no disciplinary procedures, nothing to mar the upward course of Swainson's career. Alec almost wondered if the file had been edited, it seemed so satisfactory, but of course the file had no interest in items of a less pleasant sort. The jealousies of his colleagues, the affairs with juniors, the coolness of his relations with his wife – these were not the business of the file, so long as they remained within moderate bounds, so long as nobody complained, or made accusations, or suffered in public. So long as no one tried to murder Dr Swainson.

Alec turned to the file on Mary Whinbush, but before he could open it there came a bang from the outer room, as if a chair had been knocked over, and a moment later Jayne Simmonds's face appeared at the door, alarm written all over it and very red.

'Sir, the Superintendent's here. Shall I show him in?'

'Please,' said Alec, but the reply was superfluous, for the Superintendent's bulk was already blocking the light and Jayne squeezed back against the doorframe to let him enter.

'Don't you go,' the Superintendent said curtly to Jayne. 'Now, who are you?'

'WPC Simmonds, sir.'

'Sir, I asked her . . .' Alec began.

'Oh, you are in the force, then, are you, Simmonds? But you're not CID are you? I know every CID man and woman in the county. You're uniformed branch.'

'Yes, sir.'

'Then you're improperly dressed, aren't you?'

'Sir,' Alec said firmly, 'I asked WPC Simmonds to come in plain clothes, so that she could be less conspicuous in her work here.'

'You mean you've been using a uniformed officer for CID work on your own authority?'

'Yes, sir. That's right.'

'Right, well, you, Simmonds, can get straight back to the police station and take up your normal duties. You are not a CID officer. You will change straight back into uniform and if I see you on duty in plain clothes again I shall discipline you for being improperly dressed.'

'Yes, sir.' Jayne Simmonds's face was white, now, but resolute.

'That'll be all.'

'Yes, sir.' Alec realized she was seething with anger and it was with relief that he saw her turn to go. Arguing with the Super in this mood would be suicidal.

'I might have realized,' the Super began, not waiting until WPC Simmonds was out of earshot, 'that by calling unannounced I would find everything in a right mess, but I didn't think even you would have the nerve to use uniformed branch for CID work without referring the matter to me for my authority, which would not have been given.'

'I needed a woman officer, sir, for some of my inquiries.'

'Then get one through the usual ways. We do have women CID officers, you know, Stainton. For Christ's sake, why I ever agreed to let you stay on this case I do not know. You realize we've had complaints about you every day so far? Asking for trouble, that's all it was, letting you loose on this case. You're supposed to be working to me, clearing everything, so we can avoid balls-up like this.'

'Sir, you have had my report first thing each day.'

'And it's next to useless.'

'If you've no confidence in my handling of the case, sir, then I'd rather not go on with it. I'll say that in my next report, if you like.'

'Don't you get uppity with me, my lad. Oh, I know about your little chats with the ACC. You're his blue-eyed boy, I know. So you think the Super's just an absolute sod you have to put up with till your meteoric career takes you beyond his orbit. Well, let me tell you, whatever you may do in the future, at the moment it's my job to try and turn you into a detective. I don't want people going round telling everyone how I trained a prat who can't open his mouth without putting his foot in it. That's why I have those reports every day, and that's why, believe it or not, I read them, every word. All right. What've you been doing today?'

Alec outlined his researches into the alibis, the conversation with Miss Carmel, and the sifting through the personal files.

'So you think he was with her on Friday night?'

'It seems probable, sir. I think she'll admit it sooner or later.'

'Make it sooner. What about his other girlfriends?'

'WPC Simmonds was following those up, sir. I wanted to get hold of them and find out what they could add to the picture of Dr Swainson for us.'

'Hm. Nothing more from the doc?'

'Nothing yet, though he's following things up informally.'

'You think something rendered him unconscious? That wouldn't have shown up on the PM?'

'That's right, sir, though I can't imagine what. They didn't find any evidence of drugs, no sign of a blow either, so either Dr Swainson was extremely obliging and got into the drawer himself . . .'

'As a joke, maybe?'

'Maybe. Or there was some other means of rendering him unconscious first, or, he was unconscious anyway and someone came across him and just took the opportunity that was offered to wipe out a score.'

'Seems chancy. I'd like it better if someone could have known he'd be out cold. Anything else?'

'That's all at the moment, sir. I did think of going over Dr Swainson's house, but the ACC thought we ought to leave it since Dr Norman was away and couldn't give her consent.'

'Rubbish. This is a murder inquiry – at least, I suppose

it is. Homicide, anyway. All right, asking nasty questions isn't going to make you any friends, but it's no good pussy-footing around.'

Alec thought of the Super's earlier reaction to his interview with Dr Norman and decided he was regretting having claimed to know her quite so well. Or maybe he was just a good cop, who put things like that aside for the sake of solving the case.

'Right.' The Superintendent got heavily to his feet and turned for the door.

'I want those reports on my desk every morning first thing. I don't want any blunders. Apart from that, keep at it. Lean on the secretary a bit. If Swainson was last seen by her it's an important matter. And sort out the medical side more thoroughly. Routine, Stainton. Check and re-check. See if Swainson – ' Alec noted it was no longer "Dr Swainson" now – 'was drawing any drugs from the hospital pharmacy. With two doctors in the family, he'd hardly trouble his GP and he may have been on something and took too much.'

The Super ploughed through the outer office, Alec in his wake. 'Other than that, you're doing all right. Get Simmonds back here,' he said unexpectedly, adding sarcastically, 'I'll authorize it. But get her in uniform. And if she does anything out of uniform, whether it's plain clothes or just her bra and knickers, just make sure I don't know about it. That's something I can't authorize, and I won't. OK? Right.'

Alec breathed deeply and watched through the window as the Superintendent made his forceful way towards the footpath, then he returned to his own room and reached for the phone, glancing at his watch.

WPC Simmonds had not arrived back at the police station, so Alec left a message that she was to come straight back to the hospital as soon as she had changed into uniform, and asking her to pick him up a sandwich on the way. Then he reached for the file on Mary Whinbush which he had set aside when the Super made his entrance.

The file was a thin one, charting a steady though relatively brief career at the hospital, with notes of previous jobs, back to the time Mary had left school at the age of sixteen. Surprisingly, it seemed Mary had been married briefly, though there was no record of why the marriage had ended. At any rate, Mary was now single for tax purposes. Alec pushed the file on to the pile at the edge of the desk. That left just Miss Carmel's own file and, with a feeling that it was bound to be heavily edited and disappointing, Alec slid it towards him.

It was neither. So far as Alec could see, it was painfully complete – perhaps there was a duplicate somewhere, so that deletions would be obvious. Painfully, because it recorded Josephine Carmel's dismissal from her previous job as accountant with a local firm. Reasons were not given, and if there had been a criminal charge involved it would probably be beyond the time after which details could be erased from the records. Guarded and disappointed references, however, made it plain that financial deceit had been involved and hinted at a generally unsatisfactory conduct which seemed grotesquely at odds with the calm, efficient Josephine Carmel who was secretary of Ovenden Hospital. Alec wondered how she had got such a responsible post with such an unsatisfactory record, but the file gave no clues. Had some friend pulled strings, or had there been a deliberate policy to give a fresh start to someone who had fallen? It certainly seemed surprising that she had not first had to prove her trustworthiness in less important positions.

So, had there been lapses? Had Miss Carmel sat down

and coolly set about defrauding the Health Authority in some way which Swainson had come to know about? Swainson was in no position to tell him.

Meanwhile, there was something else he had to check.

Chapter Seven

DC Johnson was surprised to be asked to accompany the Inspector over to the mortuary, but the change from the stuffy heat of the office was welcome. Alec left Jayne Simmonds, trim and severe in uniform again, poring over her notes and ringing a succession of telephone numbers in search of Swainson's lovers.

The mortuary, shaded by trees, was cool, and the inner room more so. An aura of dust and disuse had settled over it again now that the two bodies had been removed. Trapped flies buzzed half-heartedly against the window-panes, otherwise all was silent.

'Now, you're here in the first place as a guard against accidents,' Alec said, making for the row of doors which masked the refrigerated compartments. He reached for the handle of the bottom left-hand drawer and swung it open.

'What I'm going to do,' he said, turning so that his back was to the drawer, 'is pretend I'm Dr Swainson and that I've gone off my head. Probably you think I have, but we'll let that one pass for now. So I'm going to pretend that just for a joke, or something, I get myself into this drawer – ' he put his palms on the base of the drawer and with a little jump sat himself up on it, as on the edge of a table, 'and then am fool enough to slide myself – ' he lay down on the drawer and reached above his head for the top of the door opening, 'into the fridge.' Alec pulled himself back into the fridge as far as he could, then by pushing with the palms of his hands on the roof of the compartment he managed to slide himself in until only his feet were projecting.

'That's as far as I can go. Am I right in?'

'You've still got your feet out, sir.'

'Right.' Alec's voice was muffled. 'Push me in.'

Johnson grasped the handles of the sliding drawer, but it stuck in its runners and to help it he tentatively pushed on the soles of Alec's shoes. The drawer disappeared.

'OK, how do I shut the door?' Alec said. There was a heaving and pushing from inside the compartment and Alec's foot waved in the air as he tried to hook the door shut. 'Pull me out again.'

Back in the light, Alec sat up on the shelf, pushing the hair back out of his eyes.

'Whew. I'm glad that was impossible. It'd be an awful way to do yourself to death. Even without the door shut it gives you a very nasty sensation indeed. Why did you push the soles of my feet?'

'It stuck on the sliding bit, sir. Sorry.'

'No, that's fine. Just made me wonder. Right, so that's not really on. Well, we thought it wasn't, but it's as well to be sure. Now experiment number two.'

Alec went through to the outer room and sat at the desk. Suddenly, he gave a moan and slumped forward, one arm outstretched, his cheek against the desktop.

'OK, now you, Andy, have got to get me into the drawer without any help from me, and without leaving any clues. Off you go.'

Johnson surveyed the problem for a moment, then took the outstretched arm and swung it over his own shoulder. With a smooth movement he straightened up, bringing Alec with him. The chair, caught behind Alec's knees, fell over backwards with a crash. With one arm round Alec's waist and holding tightly to Alec's arm with the other hand, Johnson staggered through to the inner room,

Alec's shoes dragging limply over the floor. When they reached the open drawer, Johnson swung round and with a hitch of the shoulders let Alec's weight down till he was half sitting on the open drawer. Easing him carefully till he was recumbent, Johnson swung Alec's legs up after him. Alec lay reasonably straight, on the shelf and Johnson reached to slide the drawer shut. Alec sat up quickly.

'OK, we'll draw the line there. I don't know that I fancy the inside of that place again, it's a bit chilly for my taste. Good. We know that can be done, and it didn't seem to take very long, either.'

'It'd be a bit of a task for someone who wasn't used to handling bodies, sir. Getting you up on the shelf, that was the tricky part.'

'Right. What about scuff marks from the shoes on the floor? Scene of crime didn't find any. That suggests someone picked him up bodily, maybe.'

'Could be, sir. Or took his shoes off first.'

'Ah, quite so. Let's wander back, shall we?'

They returned to the makeshift office to find Jayne Simmonds writing up her notes with a satisfied expression. All three of the women Mary had spoken of had been located, and all were close enough to be visited from Ovenden. One, Margaret Bickerstaff, who had been a radiographer at Ovenden, had given up work just before the birth of her first child two years earlier and was now just returned from hospital after a second birth. Lindsey Welch, who had been a staff nurse when Swainson took an interest in her, had since managed to be both married and divorced, and worked as an administrator at a children's hospital fifteen miles away. The last of the three, Dr Ann Ringer, had been hardest to track down although the most recent to have left Ovenden. She too was still in the same health authority region, and she too was married.

Jayne had spoken to none of the women directly.

'Right, well done. I think you can get on to each of them straight away and arrange for us to call. This afternoon or tomorrow. Andy, will you fix for Jayne and me to call on Miss Carmel this evening. Me – I'm going to do some thinking,' and he went through into his office and shut the door.

Twenty minutes later Madge Bryant, rearranging the bottles on the shelves of the hospital pharmacy, was a little put out, not to say puzzled, by the appearance at the counter of a young man in a formal suit.

The pharmacy at Ovenden was neither extensive nor very busy, dealing mainly in sedatives for the elderly and painkillers for those in labour. In consequence, Madge Bryant sometimes felt insufficiently appreciated. Staff at Ovenden, she was sure, underestimated the skill and knowledge that she had to have, the heavy burden of responsibility which lay on all who handled dangerous drugs. She lived in hope that some crisis would turn the spotlight on her work and bring her the recognition appropriate to her position. So far, the pharmacy had not been broken into by a knife-toting junkie in search of a fix, neither had Ovenden turned out to be the only hospital in the country to hold supplies of some dramatic cure, and she had to content herself with ticking off the doctors for their sloppy handwriting, submitting proposals to the Health Authority for new designs of requisition forms and endlessly rearranging her stocks in accordance with a new system.

Typically, Madge Bryant's response to Alec's warrant card was to ring Josephine Carmel to inquire whether she knew of this man 'purporting to be a police inspector', having first taken the precaution of locking the pharmacy and meanwhile keeping a sharp eye on Alec for signs of trembling or dilated pupils. Reluctantly, she put the phone down.

'I can let you have ten minutes,' she conceded.

'Thank you,' Alec said mildly. 'That's very helpful of you.'

Not without many interruptions on the pharmacist's part, and much polite insistence on Alec's, he inquired about the habits of the medical staff regarding the drawing of drugs for their own use. Predictably, Miss Bryant had a strongly developed sense of confidentiality where information of this sort was concerned, but Alec set himself to inveigle her with a sense of the importance of her testimony, letting her understand that she might fulfil the role of key witness if anything untoward should come to light as a result of his questions. Miss Bryant became more forthcoming.

It transpired that most of the doctors used the hospital pharmacy as a matter of convenience when they wished to draw the usual minor drugs for themselves or their families, and that most of them caused Madge Bryant grief and trouble by their slack way with prescription forms. Nor did they appreciate that drugs were expensive. Miss Bryant suspected that they came for fresh supplies when they still had plenty left at the back of their bathroom cabinets which they were too lazy to look for.

But of course, Alec said, these were the usual little matters of aspirin and antibiotics. No doubt for anything which wasn't routine most of the doctors would go to their own GP?

Well, yes, Miss Bryant agreed. Doctors were like anyone else in wanting to have someone else's opinion on their condition, and were notoriously bad at treating themselves or their families. Why, there was a case not so long back . . . but then, that was really confidential, there had been quite a scandal at the time. Well, you

113

would have thought a paediatrician would recognize whooping cough.

So it was only the minor, everyday stuff that the doctors used the pharmacy for? And other hospital staff, of course, wouldn't be able to use it at all?

Of course not, only the doctors could write prescriptions, though that was not to say that there weren't cases where doctors did favours for others. There were some doctors who came more frequently. One of them, it emerged, was diabetic. Well, the pharmacy was of course the obvious place to come for something like that where there was a repeat prescription. Same with iron tablets and vitamin supplements when there were, well, women's troubles. Alec suppressed a resigned sigh. Did, er, any of the women draw supplies of the Pill from the pharmacy?

No. Well, it wasn't to be expected. Miss Bryant gave the impression that contraception was some form of socially taboo disease, but Alec got the picture. You came to the pharmacy if it was merely a matter of convenience. If it was a matter of confidentiality, you went elsewhere.

Someone like Dr Norman, he asked, married to another doctor – would she still go to a GP if need be, or would her husband fulfil that role?

Well, he might do, but not if Dr Norman had any sense, in Miss Bryant's view. It must be ten years since Dr Swainson had done anything more than stare down a microscope at a blood sample. You'd hardly go to him if you were actually ill, said Miss Bryant scathingly.

And vice versa. Dr Swainson wouldn't turn to his wife if he was worried about his blood pressure?

Hardly. Not with Dr Norman spending all her time on, well, what she did. Though perhaps it would be a good thing if she applied her learning to her own situation before trying it on others. Physician, heal thyself, was a good saying, in Miss Bryant's view, but when Alec delicately invited her to elaborate she retreated into maddening professionalism.

Anyway, Dr Swainson and his wife were not among those who drew any regular drugs from the hospital pharmacy? Nothing for hay fever, or to help them sleep, or for dizzy spells, or anything like that?

No; Miss Bryant saw very little of either Dr Swainson or Dr Norman, and managed to imply a coolness in her relations with them which reflected badly on their competence in general.

Just before he left, while Miss Bryant was still elaborating her views on the training of doctors in relation to drugs, Alec asked, 'Oh, by the way, who's the diabetic? You mentioned one of the doctors had been diabetic.'

Miss Bryant's mouth pursed as she debated whether or not to disclose the information. Sensing that she was about to opt for mystery, Alec cut in curtly.

'This is a police inquiry, Miss Bryant. If you would be so good.'

'Well, really. If you must know, it's Dr Shepherd. But I'm not sure . . .'

'Thank you, Miss Bryant,' Alec said firmly. 'You've been very discreet and very helpful.' A paradox which he left her to puzzle out for herself as he made his way back to the office, turning over in his mind what he had learnt.

With considerable tact, WPC Simmonds had arranged for them to visit that evening not the closest of the three ex-lovers of Dr Swainson, the radiographer, but the former nurse, now administrator, Lindsey Welch.

'She's the only one who's on her own. I thought it would be rather rough on the other two to be interviewed about their old lover when they were expecting their husbands back from work any minute.'

It was well after five when Alec and Jayne, the latter still in uniform, drove in through the gates of the hospital where Lindsey Welch worked.

'I'll see if she's in, sir,' the porter at the desk said, 'but she's usually gone by this time. Day staff leave at five.'

Mrs Welch was still in, and when they were shown into her office was at her desk, leafing through some papers, but whether out of duty or simply for effect was impossible to say. She was a handsome, rather than attractive, woman, heavily built and, predictably, nervous. Alec reflected on the tremor of shock which must have run through each of the three women at the thought that their past indiscretions might be coming home to roost in a public and unforgiving way. He set himself to put Mrs Welch at her ease so far as he could.

'I'm not going to ask for any sort of statement from you in writing, Mrs Welch, at least not at this stage, and although you will see WPC Simmonds here making the occasional note, that is purely for my own use. I want to assure you that I have no interest in what may have happened between you and Dr Swainson except as it may have a bearing on his death.' He smiled. 'So it's unlikely that I shall want to make things very public.'

He saw the desire to believe him struggle with scepticism in Mrs Welch's face and win.

'Would you like to let me have an account of your relationship with Dr Swainson, just in your own words? I'll prompt you if there's anything special I want to ask.'

The initial approach, it seemed, had come from Swainson. He had been direct, though not rude, in expressing his interest in Lindsey, who at the time was a recently qualified staff nurse on the maternity ward. She gave them to understand that this was not the first affair she had had, so that when Swainson's approach came she considered it with interest and some care. She had no

116

illusions – and Swainson had not misled her – that it was a romance, or that he would leave his wife for her, or anything of that sort. He presented it as an arrangement between adults who were frankly attracted to each other and could indulge their attraction without hurting others.

At the time, Lindsey was living in a shared house nearby, rather than a nurses' home. 'I wonder, now, whether that wasn't the attraction for him,' Mrs Welch said wryly. 'I expect he'd done his homework. He was a meticulous man. Anyway, it meant a certain freedom to come and go, and he could stay the night, of course, which he did quite often.'

'Did you ever meet in the hospital buildings? There's quite a lot of empty accommodation at Ovenden, isn't there?'

'No. There wasn't so much empty then as there is now, of course, but there was nowhere we used as a habit, so to speak. And never for sex. He wasn't the sort of person who would seize a casual opportunity, he much preferred things to be properly ordered. There wasn't much impulsiveness about him. More's the pity.'

'You never met in the mortuary? I'm sorry if that sounds in bad taste, but it is a building which isn't used much.'

'And it's the one where he was found, isn't it? No, he never suggested it and I don't know whether I'd have agreed if he had.'

'Excuse my asking, Mrs Welch, but was Dr Swainson a straightforward lover?'

Mrs Welch laughed. 'Did he want me to dress up, you mean, or tie him down? No. I expect he saw enough of uniforms during the day. He was really a very ordinary person, Inspector. In fact – ' Mrs Welch looked puzzled – 'looking back, I wonder quite why I went along with him for so long.'

'Was Dr Swainson . . . did he have any sort of condition, illness, anything, when you knew him? Did he take any tablets for blood pressure, anything like that?'

'He did take something. What it was, I can't remember, if I ever knew. Nothing he made a song and dance about, but he'd have a little bottle of something that he'd take each night.'

Alec felt the excitement of the chase well up in him, but there was nothing else Mrs Welch could tell him about Dr Swainson's tablets and he saw the quarry edge away into cover again. Now, however, he knew it was there. He had the scent.

Finally, Alec asked tactfully about the marriage, which had ended so soon in divorce.

'He thought I was being unfaithful. He found out about the others, before we were married, and convinced himself they were still going on. The ironic thing was, I was perfectly happy when I married. Didn't need anyone else. Well, he never believed me and the whole thing went sour. It didn't take long.'

'Do you know how he found out about your earlier lovers? Did you tell him yourself?'

'No. Perhaps it would have been better if I had. Some busybody must have let on.'

'You don't think he heard it from Dr Swainson himself? A sort of boasting?'

'No, why should he? All Geoffrey wanted was a quiet, steady affair, just like married life, really, and when we parted we did so on good terms. I'm sorry he's dead. I'd like to say that he'll be missed, but it wouldn't be true. Not many people will notice he's gone.'

Alec and Jayne left the hospital in mixed spirits. The information that Dr Swainson had been taking pills, even so long ago, was something of a breakthrough. But, Alec reflected, I hope when I go I get a better epitaph than that. Poor Swainson.

'Poor girl,' he said aloud. 'Let that be a lesson to you against the promiscuous life.'

Jayne Simmonds coloured. 'Yes, sir.'

'Sorry, silly thing to say, and very rude. Forget it. I just felt sorry for them both.'

'I know what you mean. That story about the pills, sir, were you expecting it?'

'Let's say I was hoping for it. Of course, he may have had something then which was purely temporary. Hay fever, or constipation. Come on, let's get back.'

Alec planned to call at Ovenden en route to Miss Carmel's house. For a start, he wanted to include this latest snippet of information in his day's report. Then there was the possibility of fresh developments while they had been out. Lastly, there was the hope of a quick bite in the canteen before they went out again.

'Sorry about the row with the Super,' Alec said as they drove back. 'That was my fault, I'm afraid.'

'That's all right, sir. He's a bit of a martinet, isn't he? There's hardly anyone in the county who hasn't been torn off a strip by him at some stage. I'm sorry he was able to use me to get at you.'

'It's happened before. I can cope with it. I think to some extent he was more angry at having to lay down the law than he was at the breach itself, if you follow me. Anyway, you'd better come in uniform every day from now on. Only, perhaps you might have some civvies on hand just in case.'

'I didn't expect to get back at all.'

'It's been useful having you. I'm afraid the hours aren't so regular as the uniformed branch, though. Still, it won't be forever.'

'I don't mind, sir, honestly. I'm really glad to be on the case. The others girls all envy me like mad.'

'That's all right, then. Now, we've Miss Carmel to see again this evening. It probably means more sordid details about Swainson's sex life. It's all a bit lurid.'

'I think it's rather sad, sir. I mean, it's not as if he was some sort of satyr. He just seems to have wanted something rather ordinary, something most men would get from their wives.'

'Only he shied away from anything long-term. In marriage you can't choose just the good times, you have to accept the bad ones as well. Swainson's answer to that seems to have been to pack up and move on before it happened. Tell me, does it surprise you that, if he was so ordinary, he was able to have all these affairs? He no sooner finished one than he started another. Yet he doesn't sound a very dashing figure, does he?'

Jayne Simmonds smiled. 'I don't suppose he'd have to be. I mean, it's not always the Latin lover types women go for, is it, sir? Any more than men go for the dolly bird type. Most people settle for something a little more comfortable.'

Alec thought of the women he had known over the years. Most had been, by any standards, attractive, but none could really be regarded as comfortable to get on with. Was that the reason none of the relationships had lasted? Until Diana, he had been getting the feeling that he was a poor hand at relationships, a man for whom the challenge of winning a woman's interest was too soon superseded by boredom or irritation with her actual presence. He had, he knew, behaved badly with some of them, leaving them hurt and disappointed. Was it that he looked for the wrong qualities, where someone like Dr Swainson, undistinguished though he might be in other respects, had judged more wisely? But now there was

Diana, with whom mutual attraction had grown into mutual respect, as each discovered in the other what had been hidden at the start. Surely, with Diana, something had grown which was different in kind from what he had known in the past? For the rest of the journey Alec drove automatically, deep in his own thoughts. Had he been aware of the quiet, prolonged sideways glances which Jayne Simmonds gave him he might have been surprised at the compassion and the longing they revealed, but he noticed them not at all.

Back at Ovenden they found DC Johnson chafing at their absence which had left him, stale after the day's work, to toil on in the bleak office. He had drafted out the day's report ready for typing on Alec's return, he had filed and documented the findings so far, and he had read through each of the personal files before obediently returning them to the secretary. On an impulse, he had checked back through the Scene of Crime report for mention of fingerprints on the soles of Dr Swainson's shoes, to be rewarded only with the knowledge that there were smudged marks which might, or might not, have been made by gloved hands. He had taken a phone call from the station. Now he was bored, and his thoughts turned to an evening with his friends, a pint or two, football on the TV, and he looked at his watch increasingly often to see when he could expect the others back. Andy Johnson liked being in the plain clothes branch. He liked the status and the feeling of being where things happened, in the team that got the results. Only, they weren't getting results at present. There was no doubt that CID had its flat spots. When he had been in traffic, now – but even there, there had been long hours of boring patrols, barely enlivened by the occasional chase of a speeding motorist or by the inevitable and draining duty of sorting out motorway accidents and marshalling impatient traffic queues. Some of the lads had been rostered with a girl, which gave you something to do in the long stretches of the night, but there weren't that many girls in traffic, and Johnson had not been so lucky. Not that he credited half the stories some of his mates told. Now he had Jayne Simmonds to work with, but did he get to see her? All day she seemed to be out with the Inspector, doing the interviews and getting the trips out, the things he himself should by rights have helped with, instead of which he was stuck back at this dump fixing the paperwork. He couldn't even leave the office for more than a few minutes till the Inspector came back, couldn't so much as have a coffee in the canteen and watch the nurses. He could work out how Swainson had died, but belief in his ability to come up with the dazzling solution which would bring his name to the lips of every senior officer and ensure a meteoric rise to the top of the branch had withered somehow. He knew himself to be below the likes of the inspector, below even WPC Simmonds, in the quickness of his mind, so it somehow didn't seem quite so worthwhile trying any more. Altogether, DC Johnson wondered if he was cut out for the detective life. Perhaps it was time to think of something different. He was twenty-nine. He drew a pad of paper towards him and began to jot down some ideas.

Twenty minutes later Johnson was quickly typing out the day's report with one eye on the clock and mentally putting on his coat to go, while Alec and WPC Simmonds walked across the hospital grounds on their way to see Miss Carmel. They went on foot, as they had to the Swainsons', the better to appreciate the way the journey might be made by Miss Carmel – or by her lover. Alec was sure in his own mind of where Dr Swainson had been on the last night of his life, though he realized that there was little in the way of evidence. Yet the day had brought him perceptibly closer to Dr Swainson's footsteps and he had the feeling that this evening would bring him within sight of the end of the chase. Unconsciously he quickened his pace, and beside him Jayne Simmonds lengthened her stride uncomfortably to keep up.

Chapter Eight

There was something incongruous in seeing Josephine Carmel at home. Her composed efficiency seemed to belong to the office, and it was as if she had been transported from her natural habitat to some artificial setting when she opened the door to them in the same clothes she had worn at the hospital. She had slipped into a pair of soft shoes, Alec noted, her only concession to informality, serving only to emphasize the changed habitat – a zebra in the arctic, a kangaroo in the back garden.

The house itself was soberly furnished but with a good eye for colour and texture. There had not been much money to lay out on decorations and furnishings, Alec surmised, but what there was had been used to good effect. The impression was strangely soft and feminine, as if the secretary's astringency was left at the hospital with the files and payslips. Alec felt awkward, knowing that he had invaded a privacy that must be the more jealously guarded for being hard won. He remembered the file, the bleak details of her wrecked career, the hints of deceit, the dismissal, and marvelled at the composure with which the secretary offered them a seat and a glass of sherry. Alec declined the drink for them both, and Miss Carmel sat quietly in a chair and folded her hands in her lap.

'Well, Miss Carmel,' Alec began, 'obviously I've been reading your personal file. I realize you've been very honest in making it available to me. I'm not concerned with the unfortunate events which took place before you came to Ovenden. What I am concerned with are more recent events and there is one area, in particular, where you have been less than honest. You must have realized it would come out in the end, and now it has. You know what I'm talking about, Miss Carmel. I think Dr Swainson spent Friday night with you in this house. On Saturday, he died. It had to come out, you see, there was no point in trying to conceal it.'

Miss Carmel looked up but said nothing. Her face was pale, the skin drawn unbecomingly over the bones beneath.

Alec said, 'Will you tell me about it?'

There was a long silence, and Alec thought she was not going to answer and that he would have to be brutal, take her to the station for formal questioning, all the things he shrank from emotionally and hated to have to use professionally. Miss Carmel looked down at her hands and twisted them slowly in her lap. Then she began to speak.

'Geoffrey and I have . . . had been having an affair. You guessed as much, and it's true. It'd been going on for four months now. Oh, I know I'm only the last in a succession of women he's had. I know it wouldn't have lasted much longer, it wasn't his way. I even played the agony aunt to one of the others when he chucked her: I had my eyes wide open when I first agreed to meet him, Inspector. You don't have to be sorry for me, I'm not a wronged woman.'

She looked up. 'He wasn't here on Friday night. He ended it last week. I don't really suppose you're going to believe that, but it happens to be true.'

Alec met her eyes. 'Go on.'

'There's not much to tell. We used to spend the evening together, not going out or anything, just sitting and reading, listening to records, watching the TV. Then we'd go to bed, just like any other couple. It was the ordinariness which made it all worthwhile, you see. Not just the sex – in fact, he wasn't a great lover, though I suppose he ought to have been, he'd had plenty of practice. It was just having somebody there, not asking too much, not even giving too much. He wasn't specially attentive, or even thoughtful. He'd let you wash up on your own, even though you'd made the meal as well, while he sat and read the paper. But he was there, and he was gentle when . . . when we made love.' Alec wondered whether Swainson had decided that this was the approach that worked best, or had he simply been the man Josephine Carmel described, not wanting too much, not giving too much. Perhaps that had been what Dr Norman could not cope with.

'He came here on Friday nights?'

'Usually. Most Saturdays, too. Though he really did stay at the hospital sometimes, if he'd worked late.'

'Tell me about the pattern of events on Saturday mornings.'

'There wasn't much of a pattern, really. Usually Geoffrey'd get up first. Sometimes he'd bring me a cup of tea – not often. Sometimes we'd both stay in bed until ten or so. It didn't make any difference, nobody took much notice of when he went in, because strictly speaking he didn't have to go in at all, you see.'

'And last Saturday?'

Miss Carmel raised her eyes sharply to his. 'He wasn't here last Saturday. I told you.'

'We think he was.'

'Then you're wrong.' She shrugged.

'Tell me,' Alec said, leaving that question, 'when you heard that Dr Swainson was missing, you must have been anxious? After all, even if you say your affair was over a day or two before, any investigation into Dr Swainson's life was bound to bring it all into the open, wasn't it? The

126

health authority would have to take notice of it, wouldn't they?'

Miss Carmel hugged herself as if for warmth, and Alec wondered if she was quite well. 'It's not a case of "would", is it? They will take notice. I expect I shall have to resign.'

To Alec's dismay, tears welled up in Josephine Carmel's eyes. The effect was startling, as if a beautiful building should start to crack and crumble away. No sobs came, just the silent tears coursing down her cheeks. WPC Simmonds rose unbidden from her chair and put her arm round the secretary, pressing her gently against herself. Alec thought of the dismissal from the previous job, the years of patient efficiency which had brought this woman to her present position, and which was now being rudely swept aside by a trick of fate – or by her own compulsion to kill her lover, for after all, the secretary still stood near the top of the list of suspects for Dr Swainson's death.

As if echoing his thoughts, she said, 'You think I killed him. You think I did see him last Friday and that we quarrelled. Nobody else saw him on Saturday morning, did they? They couldn't find him when they looked for him. If he was here the night before, I must be the last person to have seen him alive, mustn't I?'

The tears had dried now and she looked at him almost in curiosity, it seemed, for his reaction. Jayne unobtrusively removed her arm and returned to her chair.

'I think you might have killed him,' Alec said slowly. 'Anyone would have to think that. But you are not the only person against whom a case might be made, by any means.'

'I am telling you the truth,' the secretary said simply.

'Mm,' said Alec noncommittally. 'Tell me, what were the tablets Dr Swainson was taking?'

Miss Carmel looked puzzled. 'He didn't take anything, did he?'

'We've been told that he did. Surely his medical record would show whether he was under any sort of treatment? You must have read that record.'

'There's nothing in it of that sort, I'm sure. I don't recall anything.'

'Think back to the nights he was here. Follow through what you used to do. Did he take anything with his meal? With his coffee afterwards? When he went to bed, perhaps, didn't he have a bottle of anything beside the bed?'

She shook her head. 'If he did have anything like that, he could easily have kept it to himself. He'd have plenty of scope to take it when I wasn't around.'

Alec left that one. 'When did you really begin to worry about Dr Swainson's absence?'

'I suppose not until Sunday night, when he still hadn't turned up at home. Not even then, much. I thought, you see, perhaps he was with some other woman. It was almost a week since we had split up and so I no longer knew what he might be doing at any particular time.' She said it without bitterness, merely with the resignation of one to whom life has been frugal in its blessings. 'Then on Monday, of course, he would have been over at the district general hospital if he was anywhere, so I left a message that he was to ring when he arrived there. But they never rang back, and anyway, within a few minutes we'd found him.'

'Just so.' Miss Carmel was dry-eyed now, talking more dispassionately of her lover's death than she had of the death of her career earlier. Suppose in some way Swainson himself had threatened that career, would she, to protect what she had won, kill? Seeing the end of the affair already in sight? The woman was quite cool enough, and clever enough, for murder, after all.

'Your key was found in the mortuary,' he said bluntly.
'You knew that?'

'I . . . knew it was missing. I was afraid it might be
somewhere like that.'

'Two questions. Did Dr Swainson ever borrow your
key to the mortuary? And at what stage over the weekend
did you visit the mortuary yourself?'

'He never asked to borrow any of my keys. If he needed
keys he could get them from reception. I don't carry them
with me, for God's sake. How many keys do you think
there are in a place like Ovenden?'

'How do you account for the key being found in the
mortuary?'

'I don't. I left it in my office on Friday, so far as I know.
What I mean is, I never gave it to anyone else, certainly.'

'But you did visit the mortuary yourself? Letting
yourself in with your key?'

'No. I came in to the hospital on Sunday, as I told you,
and put a more organized search for Dr Swainson in
hand. As part of that, I did send one of the porters over
to the mortuary, since I had been told that Geoffrey had
a crem form to fill in on Saturday. He would have taken
the key from reception. Actually, I didn't think Geoffrey
could have done the crem form, because it hadn't been
returned. The porter found nothing, of course. So you
see, I never checked my own key.'

Alec left the secretary's house disappointed. He had
hoped that a strong case was forming against her, with
Swainson spending the night with her and using her key
when he went to the mortuary in the morning, and Miss
Carmel following him over, there to render him unconscious somehow and bundle him into the mortuary
drawer. Now it was only too clear that the case was built
of straw. He had jumped from Angela Norman's lie about
her husband's whereabouts to a detailed hypothesis

129

unsupported by any real evidence. The secretary was as likely, and no more so, as she had been before their visit to be the killer.

Gloomily he accompanied Jayne Simmonds back to the hospital where their cars sat alone in the car park, and bade her a distracted good night. Jayne gave him an anxious look and opened her mouth to say something, then thought better of it, unlocked her car and drove swiftly away. Alec stood with his arms resting on the roof of his car, staring unseeingly across the deserted tarmac to the empty buildings. For the first time, he wondered wheher he had it in him to solve this crime, to draw from this morass of fact, rumour and conjecture a solution which was not only plausible, but true. Wearily he straightened up, climbed into the car and drove away.

'This isn't like you,' Diana said, handing Alec a drink.

He roused himself. 'Sorry. Tell me about your day.'

Diana took her own glass and curled up on the big floor cushion beside the fireplace. 'The usual.' She shrugged. 'Everyone fighting for the biggest slice of the cake at the staff meeting. Had a deadly seminar with my second years this afternoon. How they even got to university, let alone hope to come out with a degree, beats me. And they're all so utterly conventional. All the business we had when we were students about fighting the establishment – it all seems to have evaporated. Agreed, they're more liberal in some ways, I mean, they take for granted things which we fought for, but as for fighting themselves to go any further, well, they're just not interested.'

She watched Alec beneath her dark lashes for signs that the tensions were relaxing, and her chatter faltered to a halt. Used as she was to the casual competence with which he customarily dealt with problems at work and upsets at home, Diana found it disturbing to see Alec depressed and unsure. For the first time she felt he might be inaccessible, that there might be a place within him where he, like everyone, was torn by self-doubt and fear of failure, and that that place might be beyond her reach. Usually, when she came home discouraged with the day or raw from some bitter encounter, it was Alec who sat beside her and patiently gentled her through, and the days when he was not there, when he was working late or overnight, were hard to take. But even harder, she now realized, would it be whenever he himself was in need of relief and comfort for he wouldn't allow himself to take it. She watched as he finished his drink and stared into the glass.

Diana stretched out her arm for him to join her on the floor cushion. He came reluctantly, sitting carelessly with his back against the wall, his legs clumsily out before him. Instinctively, Diana twisted round so that she was curled against him and it was he who offered comfort and protection, and she felt with relief some slackening of his tenseness as he began to caress her rhythmically.

At times like these, it seemed too daunting a task to be, and stay, so much in sympathy physically, mentally, emotionally, as she wanted to be with Alec. Being in love, a state which in her case had slowly overtaken her rather than arriving like a thunderbolt, brought the impulse to do and be everything that Alec needed perfectly attuned and at one, but she knew with stark realism that being in love was an exceptional state, one that must inevitably be superseded by the need to choose to love, and she was troubled by the fear that she might be unable to sustain love of that sort. She knew that for Alec, their relationship was on that footing already. He was loving because he liked and respected her, enjoyed her presence and wanted to respond to her needs; he was not in love, as she was with him, and for this she envied him. Yearning for total communion, she knew that at times she tried too hard. Now, this evening, when she still felt such an amateur at the business of living with someone, this new factor, this evidence of Alec's inner reserve, was thrown into the equation. She had tried in the past to teach him to rely on her and had been hurt that he so rarely needed to do so. This evening she realized that at the deepest level he was simply not prepared to accept her help. She felt Alec tug at the waistband of her shirt as he slipped his hand under the fabric to caress the skin at the base of her spine, and cursed herself for wearing tights, which she knew Alec abhorred. Of such small things are evenings made or broken.

'Tell me why it's been so awful today,' she said, pulling away a little so that she could look into his face.

Alec drew in a deep breath and let it out slowly. 'I don't know. Actually, in many ways it hasn't seemed so bad, at least, it didn't at the time. I seem to be walking through treacle, though, trying harder and harder to move and getting nowhere. Murder inquiries are like that. I've seen them before, it shouldn't surprise me. I suppose I thought I could make it different and slice through the entanglements by the power of naked intellect.' He laughed tiredly. 'I dare say that's why they gave me the job. The Super knew it would take me down a peg. Perhaps he hopes I'll have to confess defeat and ask for help. He may yet be right.'

'You don't really think that,' Diana said, half questioning.

Alec smiled. 'Maybe not. At least, not yet. But it's the side of detective work I hate, the sheer chore of it. Fortunately, there is the other side.'

'The people involved?'

'Mm. Though even that's a bit of a poser in this case. The trouble is, the man who's died, Dr Swainson, was so

. . . suitable a candidate, if you know what I mean. People either damn him with extremely faint praise and are unlikely in three weeks' time to remember who he was, or they very definitely resent him.' He told Diana about the stale formality of the marriage with Dr Norman, the bitterness of Josephine Carmel and Lindsey Welch.

'You can't say he was really the cause of their misery, surely?' Diana asked. 'After all, he did at least give them something – companionship, sexual love. It was hardly his fault the nurse's marriage broke up, for instance.'

'Wasn't it? I don't know. It does seem that everyone he touched had their lives made miserable, while he got precisely what he wanted. Maybe it's the sheer selfishness I hate. Oh, sure, they all went in with eyes open and so forth, he took advantage of no one in that sense, but everyone ended up dancing to his tune to provide him with the life he wanted, at no cost to him – the cost was always to themselves. Now he's dead, perhaps because someone found the cost too high, I can't help feeling less than wholehearted about tracking down the murderer. If only one could avoid understanding people. Even that wretched chap Ingham, who's as twisty as they come and stuck up with it, you can't help feeling that if you were in his shoes, conscious of your own failure, short of money – oh, I know it's his fault if he's overspent – but it would make anyone twisted and unlikeable.'

'But you can't take that into account. You can't weigh the merits of the victims and the murderers, Alec. How many men have done society a service, in that light, by doing away with a nasty character? But society's had to catch them and punish them, all the same. It's the only way you can have anything approaching justice. Like that peer they hanged at Tyburn, Lord Ferrers, was it? – just to show people that they were determined the law should apply to everyone equally. I suppose,' she added, 'you really have ruled out everything except murder in this case?'

'Unless it's something we really can't imagine. Only, it isn't really murder, I don't think. Is it murder when you don't actually kill someone, but you make it virtually certain they will die all the same?'

'It was an awful way to die, Alec. That should make your job easier. He may not have been a nice man, but you wouldn't wish that sort of death on anyone. It was all in the paper, at least, probably not all, but enough. Don't you usually keep something back that only the murderer could know, so that you could trap him with it?'

'Mm. Except it may well be a woman in this instance.'

'Swainson's wife, for instance? What's she like?'

'That's another poser. Unsympathetic, as far as her general approach goes, always on her high horse and trying to put you down. She reduced one of our WPCs to a spot of grease simply by trapping her in a very deep armchair. The funny thing is, I think if you knew her in other circumstances, you might quite like her. Not as a wife, though. I fancy it would be rather like being married to a praying mantis, you'd start to feel insecure as each mealtime approached.'

'You realize what her job is at the hospital?'

'Family planning, yes.'

'And venereology. Sexually transmitted diseases, problems with frigidity and performance and what-not. Other people's habits, all those tests and examinations; it's hardly surprising if she's not the most comfortable woman to have around.'

'The thing is,' Alec said, 'was she like that to start with, or did she pick it up as a speciality as some sort of reaction to her own marriage? Which came first? And why should we assume she isn't as clinical and dispassionate about it as any other doctor? After all, it's a legitimate speciality and it meets a real need. You accept the same thing in a male gynaecologist easily enough.'

'Mm. I know, it's irrational. You just can't help thinking it must reflect some flaw in her own make-up, or in her own marriage. She's your most likely suspect, I suppose?'

Alec scratched his head and Diana took the opportunity to change her position and ease a cramped leg.

'Well, she certainly was number one, though you have the problem of why she should want to get rid of him now, when she could presumably have done so ages ago. I'm sure she'd known about the affairs for years. And then there's the fact that she seems to have an alibi for most of Saturday, though we haven't checked it through fully yet. Did she know where Dr Swainson would be? She tried to contact him, you know, so far as we know without success. Of course, that could easily be a blind. It'd be convenient if it were her, but we really don't have any grounds for thinking that it might be, apart from a general distaste for the woman and the fact that it so often is someone close like that. There are plenty of other candidates with as good a case against them: Ingham, for one, whose where-abouts are still unclear, Carmel for another because she was the latest mistress and things had come to an end, and she had a record anyway. Then there's anyone Swainson met, or planned to meet, on Saturday morning. That might be Ingham, possibly, or Carmel's planned replacement. Shepherd, if there really was something fishy about the death of her patient. Whoever you look at, you can make out a case against them, but only if you give excessive weight to speculation. In hard practical terms there is so far no case worth the name against anyone. And that is what I find so dispiriting. If we're still like this at the end of the week we've probably had it.'

'What's the next step?'

'Interviews, and more interviews. And if they don't want to tell us things, we can't make them, unless we get enough of a case to pull someone in for formal questioning. So far as the question of how he died goes, we've this matter of the pills to follow up.'

'What could they be, that wouldn't show up at the post-mortem?'

'What indeed? They may have been simply something he took for hay fever, or indigestion, something he took in the past and nothing to do with his death. Then again, if he was taking something, why didn't we find the container? The more you push for answers, the more questions you uncover. It's like wrestling with an octopus.'

'Have you ever wrestled with an octopus?' Diana asked innocently.

'All right, clever clogs. How about something to eat?'

Diana, ready though she sometimes was to resent being cast in the role of domestic servant, recognized that this was not the time and scrambled to her feet.

'Devilled eggs do you?'

'Lovely.' He smiled. Sometimes he liked to sit and just watch Diana moving about the flat, poised and purposeful. On occasions, he would encourage her to do so *en deshabille*, for the sheer pleasure of her body, but somehow not tonight. The reason was obvious, of course; this bloody case was turning everything sour for him, so that even what was normal and wholesome seemed shabby and dubiously motivated. Was Swainson casting his influence even beyond the grave? Had someone else, sensing this same distaste with innocuous pleasures, felt that the world would be well rid of the man who could so taint the lives of others? Well, it was Alec's responsibility to find out, but not tonight. The evening, and there was little enough left of it, in all conscience, was for refreshment and recuperation. Tomorrow would suffice for resuming the chase.

Later, as they lay in bed, Diana said, 'Alec, are you going to stay with your job? With the police?'

There was a long silence, in which she stared up at the darkness, waiting for his answer, knowing what it must be.

'Yes,' he said at last.

'There are so many other things you could do instead. Especially with your contacts. And you'd be good at them. You'd be good at whatever you did.'

'And I could be free of irritating scruples and moral dilemmas? Maybe. Maybe I believe in your form of justice, the peer and the commoner all being subject to the same law, a law which we're struggling to uphold. And usually just managing to do so.'

'I hate it when you take so much out of yourself. And out of me.'

'It'll get easier. If I do well, move up the ladder, I'll be insulated and someone else will face the conflicts for me. There'll be more administration, more theoretical decisions, more questions of strategy and fewer of tactics.'

'You'll be good at that. Being wise. I just hate you having to do what you do now.'

'Perhaps it's something I have to go through, in order to be any good later.'

Diana said, 'It must have been worse with the death penalty. Knowing you could send someone to their death.'

Alec thought of Josephine Carmel, of Dr Shepherd, or Dr Norman, with a noose around the neck, subjected to the dismal rituals of institutionalized killing in some windowless cell block. 'It wouldn't make any difference,' he said. Was that true? Could he find it in him to be the agent of someone else's death, even with the approval and sanction of society? Too easily. As easily as now he could pursue Miss Carmel, Dr Norman, Dr Ingham, to the degrading world of slopping out and standing to attention, of no privacy and of petty privilege. You didn't let yourself see it like that. You kept it deliberately simple, ingenuous, unthinking; all the habits of mind Alec had acquired over his thirty years, all the attributes he admired in Diana and shared with her, had to be deliberately put off in order that it should be possible to function in this job. You had to have a very strong conviction of the worth of the job so to subsume your very nature to it. A very strong conviction indeed.

Alec sighed, and pulled Diana closer, moulding her body to his in the darkness, and closed his eyes. For Diana, however, sleep would not come so readily, and she lay a long while staring into the darkness at the phantoms which wouldn't go away.

Chapter Nine

'Right,' Alec said. 'I want you to check every source in the area where Dr Swainson might have obtained supplies if he was taking some sort of regular medicine. The pharmacy here we've already dealt with. There's the pharmacy at the district general hospital, also check any other hospital Swainson went to on a regular basis, say to deliver lectures or for committee meetings. Then there are the dispensing chemists, starting with those nearest his house. Don't forget the prescription could be in his own name, or that of his wife, but if it's the sort of thing I think it might be then it'll be a regular visit, maybe every week, maybe every month, every three months even, I don't know. Then fix with Ingham for him to come here this afternoon. We'll see him on our own ground this time, I think. Go back over Dr Norman's movements on Saturday and summarize them, with any discrepancies highlighted – put that on my desk. And see if you come up with any sightings of unusual characters hanging round the mortuary area on Saturday morning. If Swainson met someone there, or he intended to, that might make that person the last to see him alive. That keep you out of trouble for a bit?'

DC Johnson nodded, his heart sinking. Another day of slogging away in the office. Another day of paperwork and routine instead of being out at the sharp end with Inspector Stainton, a role which he knew would be filled by Jayne Simmonds. Of course, it was hardly to be wondered at that the Inspector liked to monopolize her company. Any other officer would have done the same.

But up to now, Johnson had always thought the Inspector to be different from any other officer. To find him as flawed and predictable as everyone else was a disappointment. Galling, too, to think that those charms which WPC Simmonds was so chary of dispensing to mere constables would probably be freely surrendered to an up-and-coming inspector. Maybe in a year or two he himself would be in Alec's position. Maybe.

'Jayne, brief me on this woman we're going to see,' Alec said, and thought: Good Lord, I sound like a TV cop. What's got into me today?

'Well, sir,' WPC Simmonds began, 'so far there's not a lot to know. She worked here up to about two and a half years ago, then she left to start a family. Happily married, at least I presume so, just had the second child. When I spoke to her on the phone she sounded very sensible. Not really surprised to hear from us, just anxious in case we were going to start raking up the dirt.'

Alec went over to the window and gazed out. A little procession wended its way along one of the paths that, web-like, linked the blocks. A nurse, walking slowly backwards, glancing over her shoulder occasionally, meanwhile encouraging a shuffling, dressing-gowned old man with a walking frame. Bringing up the rear, a bored porter, bending down to pick up a cigarette packet, throwing it aside.

Alec shuddered, and thought of the woman he was to interview. She must have thought herself free at last of Swainson's influence, able to turn instead to her husband, her family. Was he now to make her a sacrifice to the dead consultant?

'Let's get it over with,' he said, half to himself, and turned back to Jayne Simmonds. She was standing watching him with a puzzled frown, and he made himself smile and said, 'OK, let's go.'

Margaret Bickerstaff was as sensible as WPC Simmonds had said, and more so than Alec had dared expect. The Bickerstaffs' modern semi stood on an estate on the far side of town, and was trim without being fussed-over – a description, Alec thought, that could be applied to Mrs Bickerstaff herself. A short, slim woman, still in her twenties, Alec judged, she opened the door to their ring with a politeness underlain by habitual warmth. Warning them to beware of toys on the floor, but without apology, she led them into a pleasantly lived-in sitting-room and offered them a seat while she brewed coffee. Alec looked about him, noting the television pushed well out of the way, the cloth-backed children's books on the bottom shelf of the bookcase, a catholic selection of paperbacks above. On the far wall hung an amateurish watercolour, clearly for its associations rather than for effect. Altogether, Alec felt that Mr Bickerstaff, wherever he might be, could feel fortunate in having such a home to come back to.

'Where does your husband work?' he asked, as Margaret Bickerstaff returned with a tray and coffee things.

'He's at the local comprehensive, head of religious studies.' Alec felt, rather than saw, some awakening of interest in WPC Simmonds. He waited for Mrs Bickerstaff to add the conventional complaints about teachers' pay and conditions, but he waited in vain. This was a woman, he decided, whom he was going to enjoy interviewing.

She passed them coffee and placed a plate of plain chocolate biscuits within reach.

'You've come because Geoffrey Swainson's died, and you've found out that I had an affair with him.' She raised her eyes to Alec's and held his gaze.

'Yes, that's right. We're not interested in the affair as such, but there may be things that emerge from what you know of Dr Swainson which would help our enquiry. I'm sorry we have to call, but we do, and that's all there is to it.'

'I talked it over with my husband,' she said unexpectedly. 'We both agreed I should tell you everything I could and leave you to decide what may have a bearing on Geoffrey's death.'

'Your husband is a very understanding man. And a very wise one.'

'He is,' she said simply. 'He knew about Geoffrey. Oh, it was before I met him, of course, and it was a part of my life I wasn't very proud of, but we felt that if our marriage was to mean anything it had to be completely open.'

'Tell me about your relationship with Geoffrey Swainson.'

Margaret Bickerstaff sat back in the chair, and her glance strayed to the watercolour on the wall.

'I only had one love-affair before I met Richard, one serious one, I mean, and that was with Geoffrey. I'd been at Ovenden two years, so you see I'd known Dr Swainson, in the way you know everyone at a small hospital. I suppose girls often tend to size up the men they work with, you know, the ones they might fancy and the ones they couldn't. I didn't do that, I never have really, but if I had Geoffrey would have been in the second category. He didn't pursue me, or anything like that; in fact I never really thought he was aware I was there. Then something happened that upset me a lot.' She looked up at Alec. 'I don't think it has any bearing on what you want to know, and . . . I'd prefer not to go into details. It made me rebel, anyway, kick against everything I believed and lived by. It wasn't that I abandoned things I believed so much as that I felt I had to smash and overturn and spoil. Perhaps it sounds silly, but if you've ever been through it you'll understand what I'm talking about.'

'I know,' Jayne put in unexpectedly. Alec glanced at her and said nothing.

'Well, one of the ways I wanted to spoil was to have an affair. Preferably with someone I didn't care about. And there Geoffrey was. Somehow he seemed to pick up that I was ripe for an affair and he quite deliberately suggested that I should have one with him. He wasn't offensive or anything, he didn't make it out to be any grand passion, simply something that would meet our needs of the moment.'

'And you met . . . where?'

'In my flat, usually. I had a hospital flat; it was supposed to be shared but things were running down at Ovenden, they'd just opened the district general hospital, there was spare accommodation and I was there on my own. Oh, Geoffrey didn't come that often, he wasn't living there in any sense. Maybe twice a week he'd come in the evening, I'd cook us a meal, we'd go to bed. Doesn't sound terribly sinful, does it?'

'But the attraction for you was that you did consider it sinful?'

'Yes. It's not much of a basis for a relationship, is it? In some ways you could hardly call it that, more an arrangement. I didn't enjoy it. I told myself I did, but I was really forcing myself to hurt and spoil, as I said. It didn't give me much pleasure. Fortunately I soon sickened of it – of myself. Then everything happened at once. I told Geoffrey I couldn't go on, but he'd already decided to end it. I think he was piqued that I'd beaten him to it, actually. It offended his pride. And Richard came along. And I started to put things back together.'

She looked at him sadly but without self-pity, an attractive dark-haired woman, and he suddenly glimpsed the pain she had talked of, understood for an instant the urge to spoil, to give herself without love and without tenderness merely to gain her revenge on fate, to slight God. He wondered about the absent Richard who had taken her at her lowest point, had talked with her and understood and above all accepted.

'Do you want to ask me some questions? I'm sure what I've told you isn't really the sort of thing you want to know.'

'If I may, though you've been very frank, and I'm grateful.' Alec marshalled his thoughts. 'We know that at one stage in the last few years Dr Swainson was taking some tablets. We don't know what for, or whether it was something temporary that he subsequently got over. Do you recall him being on anything when you knew him?'

'Yes, he took a pill of some sort before he went to bed. He didn't like my knowing at first, but later he didn't care so much about hiding it. Perhaps he realized that I didn't give a damn about that or anything else.'

'Do you know what it was? I know it's a long time ago.'

She frowned. 'Some name like "Epsilon" or "Epilogue"? Not that, but like that. I know it was reminiscent of epilepsy, and I was surprised, because he wasn't epileptic so far as I know.'

'The name meant nothing more to you?'

She shook her head. 'Not my field, I'm afraid.'

'How did Dr Swainson get on with people in general? Or were there certain people he didn't get on with at all?'

'I think he generally had people's respect, professionally, but that was about the sum of it. Did he have any enemies? Hardly. Why should he?'

Alec said, 'Did you have any enemies yourself? Did your relationship with Dr Swainson make you any?'

'I don't know about that. I certainly didn't have many friends at that stage, but that was nothing to do with Geoffrey Swainson. Only . . . ' She paused and screwed her face up as if puzzled.

'Yes?'

'It may not be connected, but . . . About a year ago, no, it must be longer; maybe eighteen months. I had a . . . not a threat exactly, but one of those nasty phone calls. Obviously someone who reckoned I wouldn't have mentioned Geoffrey to Richard and thought there might be the chance of a little blackmail or something.'

'What form did the blackmail take?'

'It didn't, really. The call was terribly vague, you know, general threats about telling Richard. It was just after Gemma was born so they probably thought I was vulnerable to anything that'd threaten the marriage. Only, of course, I told Richard, and the next time they rang he took it and told them where to get off. I believe he reported it as well, actually,' she added apologetically. Alec made a note to check back but he knew what he would find. A record of the call, bland reassurance that they would look into it if it happened again, and when it didn't, nothing.

'Was it a man who rang?'

She shook her head. 'A woman.'

'No one you knew, of course? No, obviously. So we don't know whether it was money they were after, or what.'

'They can't have hoped to get much, if it was. The funny thing is, I had the impression she was trying to find out something, as if she thought she knew but needed confirmation.'

'As if,' Alec said slowly, 'she were gathering material to use against someone else.'

'Yes. That must mean against Geoffrey, mustn't it?'

'It might,' Alec admitted.

'Poor Geoffrey. You know, looking back, I'm not really sure which of us I'm more sorry for. It was a black time so far as I was concerned, and not one I'm proud of, but I did come through. I've got all this.' Her gesture embraced the room, the toys, the watercolour. 'He never had anything like this. Just that big cold house, and a wife who was bored with him. And his affairs. And now he's dead.'

'Where are your children this morning?'

'The little one's asleep upstairs. It'll be time for her feed soon. Gemma is with a friend. We thought it best.'

'I'm glad it's worked out for you,' Alec said. 'One other thing, and I'm sorry to hark back to it, but did you and Dr Swainson ever meet anywhere in the hopsital buildings? In particular, I'm interested in whether he made a habit of using the mortuary for his, ah, for meetings of that sort.'

'We met in various places to start with.' She smiled wryly. 'It all added to the perverse pleasure so far as I was concerned. I don't think Geoffrey was so keen. Do you know, I once made him make love in his lab. I don't think he ever really forgave me for that. The mortuary? No. Perhaps if I'd thought of it.'

What a waste, Alec found himself thinking, that Swainson should attract into his grubby affairs a woman such as this. Had she felt suitably defiled after their loveless couplings? Had it enhanced, or marred, the delight he felt sure she now found with the understanding Richard? He turned to WPC Simmonds.

'Got everything?'

'I think so, sir, thank you.'

Alec stood up. 'Thank you again for seeing us and being so open. So far as I am concerned, this has been a private talk, though there are some things, clearly, in what you have told me that I may need to disclose to others. The rest need not be broadcast. Will you give my thanks to your husband? He's a very sensible man. And a very lucky one.'

Margaret Bickerstaff flushed and smiled uncertainly, and Alec made for the door.

'Right,' Alec said, as they settled into the car and he started the engine. 'Tell me where we're heading.'

'Out to the motorway, sir, then I'll direct you.'

They had an hour's drive at least before they would reach the town where Dr Ann Ringer, the last of Dr Swainson's old flames, was now working in a geriatric hospital. Alec settled down behind the wheel, finding himself relaxed and confident in a way which contrasted agreeably with the doubts of the previous night. They were, he felt, on the track of a key factor in the consultant's death with the pills. Perhaps by the time they got back to Ovenden, Johnson would have unearthed the source of supply and they would know what it was Swainson was treating himself for which he didn't want on his hospital file. Now there was this new clue about the blackmail, and though he couldn't see how that might fit in at present, again he felt sure that it was an important piece of the jigsaw. Soon the pattern would begin to emerge and then it would only be a short while before the design was complete.

'Why did you say you knew what Mrs Bickerstaff meant, about wanting to kick out at the things she'd held on to?' he asked suddenly.

'I do. Anyone does, who's ever tried to live by the rules.'

'Surely we all do that, even if they're not always the same rules. But you don't let them dominate you. She made it such a –' he searched for the right word – 'such a significant matter, as if rules are fixed and can't be broken.'

'Perhaps they are. You talked of it being sinful, yourself.'

'Yes, in a sense. Not literally.'

'She meant it literally. To her that was the right context in which to talk about it, as sin.'

'Is that how you see it?'

'You must work it out for yourself, sir,' Jayne replied, with a shade of coolness in her voice. Thus far and no further, her tone said, does your position as my superior permit you to go. Chastened, Alec lapsed into silence that lasted till they turned off the motorway, but whenever he could he snatched little sideways glances at the policewoman beside him. He was not used to being wrong-footed, particularly by women. Jayne Simmonds had struck him from the start as being extraordinarily self-possessed; now, the hint of deeper qualities was intriguing.

Dr Ann Ringer received them in a shabby common room high under the eaves of a formidable pile which had only too plainly been designed as a workhouse. In a corner of the room, a deal table supported a television set, and a litter of back numbers of the *BMJ* and the *Telegraph* magazine, on top of which sat a plate with the remains of a take-away curry. Empty coffee mugs perched on the stained wooden arms of sagging chairs. Most of the curtains were still drawn. It was a glum, workaday environment, free of any sense of personality or human emotion. The latter, however, in full measure, shone from the face of the slim, fair girl who sat opposite Alec, a cigarette in her right hand. The emotion, he saw with interest, was hate.

Dr Ringer was not disposed to be cooperative, nor to appreciate Alec's apologies and protestations of confidentiality, the abruptness and gracelessness of her manner contrasting strangely with the pre-Raphaelite face and shoulder-length fair hair.

'Somebody's done for him, have they? Well, I don't suppose you need worry about who did it. If it's not his present mistress it'll be the one before that. One of his bloody women, anyway. Or one of their husbands.'

'I think,' Alec said mildly, 'that you were "the one before that", you know. Was it you, or your husband?'

'No, but it might have been. I mean, don't get the idea it was for lack of inclination or anything.'

Alec sought his words carefully, anxious not to discourage the flow of candour, or the flow of bitterness.

'You sound as if you don't retain any very pleasant memories of your time with Dr Swainson. Did you part on bad terms? Was he cruel to you? A selfish lover?'

'The last one, certainly. A selfish lover, you've hit it there all right. And cruel, in his way. Yes, we parted on bad terms. No reason why I shouldn't tell you, some busybody will. He was a selfish creep, was Geoff Swainson, and he took me for a real ride.'

'In what way?'

'Every way.'

'But one way in particular,' Alec persisted. 'Something that set you against him and led to the bitter break-up.'

Dr Ringer pursed her lips and looked at Jayne. Alec said, 'It's something you'd rather tell me when WPC Simmonds isn't here. Or tell her when I'm not here. Yes?'

'Oh, what the hell,' Dr Ringer said. Then, harshly, 'He gave me herpes.'

'He what?'

'Herpes. Like cold sores.' Alec looked mystified. 'Oh, for God's sake look it up. It's a sexually transmitted infection. Once you've got it, it keeps recurring. Geoff had it and he kindly passed it on.'

'Hence the anger of the women and the women's husbands.'

'You've got it.'

Jayne's head was bent discreetly over her book, her expression hidden.

'So,' Alec said, 'there was no chance of hiding from your husband the fact that you'd had a lover.'

Dr Ringer stubbed out her cigarette in a saucer. 'He knew anyway. But there's not much chance of his forgetting, now. It can be bloody painful, too.'

Alec said, 'You knew about the lovers Dr Swainson had before you. Do you think he picked it up from one of them?'

'I suppose so.'

Alec embarked on the now familiar round of questions. Where had they met, how had the first approaches been made; again he marvelled at the radar which told people like Swainson that a potential partner was available, so that Ann Ringer hardly knew whose had been the first initiative. She, too, had been in hospital accommodation, a shared house, so that although Swainson could stay overnight the affair was less settled and domestic than those with Margaret Bickerstaff and Lindsey Welch. Yes, they had used empty hospital buildings to meet in, though it seemed Dr Swainson was not entirely easy about this. No, they had never met in the mortuary. Pills? She had never seen anything, though it was quite possible Swainson had hidden them from her. Probably, even, given that she would be able to deduce the ailment from the brand name.

How had the relationship ended? She had moved away when her term in that job was over. About time, too. Geoffrey Swainson, Alec gathered, was not Dr Ringer's idea of a long-term partner. And when had she discovered about the, er . . . ?

About the clap? Almost immediately afterwards. And she'd seen an expert in that sort of thing to make sure of the diagnosis?

For the first time, Ann Ringer looked uncertain of herself, and it was, Alec thought, a big improvement. The hard-boiled look melted a little, revealing a vulnerability that rendered her far more attractive. Yes, she answered finally, she had gone to a specialist. It was always as well to get the best advice.

The specialist being?

A pause. Dr Norman.

It had to be, Alec thought. It could hardly have been a pleasant decision, though, in the circumstances. Despite a certain instinctive antipathy to this hard young woman, he had to admit an admiration for her stamina. Her view of life was unattractive, but she didn't shirk the consequences of that view. And that led to another consideration. Somehow, he could not see a blackmailer getting very far with this forthright young woman.

'I did gather,' Alec said, choosing his words carefully, 'that one of Dr Swainson's previous girlfriends had been subjected to some rather nasty phone calls afterwards. Not from him, but you know the sort of thing. I wondered whether you had had the same unpleasant experience?'

'No,' Dr Ringer said shortly. 'Those sorts of call don't bother me. Some women attract them because they're silly enough to respond to them by getting all worked up. But then, most women are their own worst enemies,' she added sweepingly.

Alec asked how she had spent the previous Saturday, and she replied without rancour that she had been on call in the hospital all weekend. And that, thought Alec, is about it. A remarkably brief and unprofitable interview to have driven so far for. As a matter of form he asked whether there was anything else Dr Ringer was aware of which might be of relevance to the inquiry.

'Could I put a question, do you think?' WPC Simmonds

struck in unexpectedly. 'You were at medical school with Harriet Shepherd, weren't you? Were you close?'

Ann Ringer's eyes narrowed. 'What's she been telling you?'

'Perhaps you would just answer WPC Simmonds,' Alec said.

'We were good friends to start with. Then Harriet began to be a bit of a bore. So I cut things off.'

'A bore in what way?'

'Too clinging. Always on about what great friends we were, always wanting to be part of whatever I was doing. Frankly, I didn't want anybody following me around like that. It was just too dog-like.'

'So the friendship cooled?'

'On my part, not on hers. I let her down too gently. I'd have done us both a favour if I'd been a bit more brutal. It was too much like some dreadful girls' boarding school – you know. Fourth Form at St Hilda's.'

'She didn't have boyfriends?'

'More's the pity.'

'And resented it when you did, perhaps?'

'Oh, she wasn't too bad in that respect. She didn't kick up a fuss. Just inclined to be a little too protective.'

Ann Ringer, Alec thought, would hardly feel herself in need of solicitous protection. Nor would she appreciate having her moves dogged so faithfully. He glanced at WPC Simmonds, who nodded.

'Right, thanks for your help, Dr Ringer. We'll leave you to get on with your work.'

He stood up. Jayne Simmonds followed suit. Dr Ringer remained gracelessly slumped in her chair, but when they were half way to the door she recollected herself and stood up, following them over to hold the door and stare after them as they made their way self-consciously down the bleak passage towards the stairs, the exit and the sunshine.

'Another one to be sorry for?' Alec said as they drove away.

'I suppose so, sir.'

'You don't sound terribly sympathetic. With Mrs Bickerstaff you were all understanding. Doesn't Dr Ringer qualify?'

Jayne smiled and shrugged. 'You're right, I'm being inconsistent to some extent. Both of them made their beds and now they're lying on them. Only one of them made something for herself that was better than the past. Dr Ringer seems set in the old way.'

'Maybe. Richard Bickerstaff must take a lot of credit for his wife's situation, I should have said. All this one's got is a painful condition she'd certainly rather be without.' Alec concentrated on overtaking a caravan labouring up a hill. 'She's deceiving herself, of course. You saw that.'

'Sir?'

'Wherever she caught herpes, it wasn't from Geoffrey Swainson. We'd have known about it from the postmortem. She may even have caught it from that husband of hers. It's a pretty safe bet that they were sleeping together before they got married. Whether they genuinely believe it came from Swainson is beside the point. For our purposes, the important thing is that it could have done – it must work out right on timing, incubation periods, or whatever, otherwise she wouldn't be able to deceive herself.'

'And if she could draw that conclusion, so could others.'

'Just so. And could also conclude that he was in a position to pass it on to any one of his sexual contacts.'

'Would that be a reason for murder?'

'Maybe. Or it might be a reason for blackmail. What

I'd really hoped we'd get from Dr Ringer, though, was something about those tablets. After all, the name would mean something to her, and it would also confirm that he was still taking them quite recently. It's a bit of a puzzle about the blackmail though. Why try Mrs Bickerstaff and not Ann Ringer?'

'Less chance of success? Disappointed by the failure of the previous attempt?'

'Maybe. It just nags me that the blackmail may be associated with Swainson's presence at Ovenden on Saturday morning. There's really no reason why they should be linked, but it's not that big a step from blackmail to murder, is it? We're not there yet, by a long chalk. Not only is it not the beginning of the end, I'm not sure it's even the end of the beginning.'

Chapter Ten

An hour and a half later Alec sat in his office chair, staler and hungrier, but with a satisfying sense of being on the track of something important. Opposite, Peter, the police doctor, leant forward in his seat and nodded.

'It fits. It certainly fits. Remember I said we would run one or two more tests? Well, we've got the reports back, and there's a slight scar on the brain – nothing much, probably caused by somebody being too rough with the forceps at birth. From your point of view, the interesting thing is that it can show up later as a tendency to fits. Might come on quite late in life, so that the earlier records wouldn't show it.'

'After his marriage, in other words, when he and Dr Norman were looking after each other's health needs.'

'Precisely. And only putting on record what they wanted to. Now, fits of this sort could be quite mild and easily controlled. You'd have to have some tablets to take on a regular basis, but that's all. In every other respect you'd live a perfectly normal and unrestricted life.'

'Could the tablets be something like "Epilogue" or "Epsilon"?'

'They could indeed. Epilim, for example. That's sodium valproate. You could take that as tablets, or as a liquid or syrup. He might get away with two tablets a day, say 1000 milligrammes, or he might have to take more.'

'And if he didn't take them?'

'Then the fits would recur.'

'Sorry to be so ignorant, Peter, but could you spell it

out for me? What sort of fits, for a start. Rolling on the ground gnashing the teeth?'

'Well, it all depends. No two people manifest in quite the same way. With this sort of minor brain damage, he could have had temporary absences, as it were, or blackouts – probably not very long in duration. He'd come round again quite quickly. There's no question of him going straight into a deep coma or anything.'

'And to have one of these blackouts, he'd have to have forgotten to take his pills.'

'That's about it. Except at the early stage, when he could get them while they were still settling the dosage.'

'This wasn't. He'd been taking the pills at least for a couple of years. Hardly seems likely, does it, that a doctor, knowing the consequences, would be slipshod over taking his tablets. We're back in the realms of substituted pills and so forth. It all seems so unlikely. Presumably, you couldn't really know in advance when he would have an attack? I mean, as a way of arranging a murder it's not only very complicated, it's also so chancy.'

'Right. Unless you stuck with him all the time, literally every minute, till he succumbed. You certainly couldn't bank on it happening between the hours of ten and eleven, for example.'

'Would they be easy tablets to substitute?'

'Come and see; they'll have some in the pharmacy, probably. By the way, there's surely another problem with the idea of substitution?'

'Where's the bottle? Yes, of course. Mind you, he might not have carried it with him. It could be with his stuff at home, in his bedside cabinet or whatnot. Wherever he spent the night.'

'Don't you believe it,' the doctor said confidently. 'It gets to be like your wallet or your house keys, always with you.'

They walked along the maze of paths towards the dispensary.

'Can you sign for this stuff?' Alec asked.

'Do you want me to? It's a bit tricky when I haven't got a patient. We can get some out and have a look at it, anyway, if Madge'll let us. Incidentally, have you started looking for where Swainson himself got the stuff?'

'Yes. We've tried all the independent chemists – no luck. Ditto one of the chains. The other chains are referring it to head office before letting us have any information.'

'It's more likely to be one of the chains. More anonymous. A smaller chemist would remember.'

'Why should he worry if they did, though?' Alec asked. 'Surely it's not the end of the world to have it known you're taking anti-epileptics?'

'You'd be surprised. Anything which smacks of mental disorder and people get all upset and start overreacting. Then again, he could lose his driving licence if he'd had a fit within the last three years. He was really being a little naughty in keeping it quiet. Irresponsible, really, and selfish.'

'He was a selfish man,' Alec said mildly, 'from what I know of him.'

Madge Bryant, the hospital pharmacist, reacted predictably to Peter's request for Epilim. There was nobody in the hopsital currently being treated with Epilim, and if there were, it was not for Peter to prescribe for them. If he wanted drugs he should draw them from the pharmacy at the district general hospital, which was his formal base. Peter explained patiently that he merely wished to see samples of the tablets, but that if she wished to make a fuss about it he would complete a prescription form. He added firmly that he was entitled to draw drugs on prescription at this hospital as at any other, and that whether or not she agreed with that right, he proposed to exercise it.

Faced with such directness there was nothing the pharmacist could do but disappear into the stockroom, which she did, emerging a few minutes later with a small plastic bottle which she reluctantly handed over. Peter unscrewed the bottle and shook a couple of tablets into his hand, holding them out for Alec's inspection.

'Not easy to fake,' Alec said disappointedly, eyeing the bright lilac tablets.

Peter shrugged. 'Not that hard, either, if you had the equipment.' He glanced wickedly at Madge Bryant, then back to Alec, and winked solemnly. 'Seen all you want to?'

'It'll be all over the hospital by nightfall,' Peter said as they turned back down the corridor, 'but there's not much you can do about that. It won't matter much to Swainson now if his little secret comes out.'

'Don't forget that to one person, at least, it wasn't a secret.'

'Angela Norman, you mean?'

'I meant the murderer, actually,' Alec said, 'but you're right, of course. Anyway, I fancy you've made your point about substitution. I have to conclude, I suppose, that something happened to prevent Swainson taking the thing on Friday night.'

'And Saturday morning.'

'And Saturday morning, just so. He forgot, or was prevailed on to give it a miss. Or, just possibly, he was already unconscious by some other means. No, we've decided it was not taking the pills that . . . oh hell, now I don't know what we have decided.'

'That he was unconscious before he went into the mortuary drawer, that's all. So you're right, he could have been unconscious some time, or he could have had a blackout through not taking his pills, a blackout which someone, by accident or design, was able to take advantage of to do away with him.'

'But anyway, where's the bottle?'

'Where's the bottle. Quite.'

'Anyway,' Alec concluded, 'the likely sequence would seem to be, blackout, fortunate discovery by person of malicious intent, Swainson gets bundled into the cooler. Swainson comes to, finds himself in the fridge, goes off his head with panic and chokes on his own vomit. That sound right?'

'Yes. It's a tight time schedule, of course, you must recognize that. He might only be out for a few minutes, maybe not even that long. And nobody would know he wouldn't come to while he was being manhandled into the fridge. That'd take a bit of explaining away.'

'But it fits the facts, so far as you're concerned.'

'I suppose so. Yes.'

'Then whoever did this lets themselves out of the mortuary, pulling the door to behind them – no problem there, it's a Yale latch – leaving the key on the floor. For some reason.'

Alec sank into gloom at the perplexities of the case, but they returned to the office to an air of eagerness which was almost palpable. Both the constables scrambled to their feet as the door opened and Alec was hard put not to laugh as they manoeuvred for his attention.

'All right,' he said with a humorous glance to Peter, 'Andy first.'

'We've got the chemist, sir,' Johnson said excitedly. He gave the name of one of the High Street chains. 'Regular prescription in Swainson's own name. Got the name of the stuff, too.' He peered at his notes. 'It's – '

'Epilim, quite so.'

'Yes, sir,' Johnson replied, crestfallen. 'They've let us

have copies of the entries.' He held out half a dozen stapled sheets, photocopied extracts from a drug register. Alec glanced at them and handed them on to Peter.

'Last prescription seems to be about a month ago. The records stop ten days back, though.'

Alec glanced at him sharply: 'Get hold of the entries for the last ten days, then.'

'Yes, sir. Sorry, sir. I should have done that.'

'OK, it's a good piece of work, anyway. What've you got for us, Jayne?'

'Well, sir,' Jayne Simmonds was eager and slightly flushed. Her hands moved restlessly until she realized what she was doing and clamped them together with a downward glance. 'You know I asked Dr Ringer about being at medical school with Harriet Shepherd.' Alec nodded. 'Well, I've been gathering more gossip. Or rather, realizing the meaning of what I've been hearing. Dr Shepherd's, she's a . . .'

'She's a lesbian?' Alec helped her out, deadpan.

'Well, it hasn't quite been put in those terms, sir, but she certainly prefers her friendships to be with women rather than men, and the friendships tend to be rather on the suffocating side. Several of the girls gave me the impression they go out of their way to avoid being on their own with her. And she apparently got very hot under the collar just after Dr Ringer left Ovenden, to the point where she was being quite offensive to Dr Swainson. Making some sort of accusation about the way Dr Ringer had been badly treated, without mentioning anything specific.'

'And you thought she knew about the herpes and was all possessive and indignant on her friend's behalf.'

'Yes, sir.' WPC Simmonds looked at him appealingly. 'It sounds a bit far-fetched, I know.'

'Not at all. Though it's only based on hearsay. Still, it's useful to know. What do you think, Peter?'

'Would she kill to avenge her lover?' He shrugged. 'Perhaps. Who can tell? We none of us know what it's like to be like that, do we? We're going well beyond the scope of normal behaviour, obviously.'

'I should be inclined to say we were doing that anyway,' Alec observed drily. He nodded to the two constables. 'Well done, anyway.'

'There's another thing, sir,' Johnson said.

'More?' Alec raised his eyebrows.

'We've found out who Dr Norman's boyfriend is.'

'Good Lord, you have been busy. How did you manage that?'

Johnson and WPC Simmonds glanced at each other.

'Well, actually, sir,' Jayne said, 'he phoned in and asked if he could speak to you.'

'And you said yes, I hope. Is he coming here?'

'We left it that we'd ring him back. He's a solicitor in Oxfordshire.'

'More driving. Well, fix me an appointment for this afternoon and I'll get over there straightaway.'

'Sir, Dr Ingham's coming in twenty minutes, don't forget,' Johnson put in.

'Right. I'd forgotten. I'll still go this afternoon, but make it later. Why can't there be more hours in the day?'

'I'll leave you to it,' the doctor said. 'Are you going tomorrow? The ACC's do?'

'What?'

'Sorry, sir,' Johnson said. 'There's an envelope on your desk which I brought back from headquarters.'

Alec glanced through to his desk, where a thick white envelope lay prominently in the centre of the blotter, and raised his eyebrows to Peter, who grinned. 'I heard you'd been invited. Better dust down your medals.'

Alec frowned. 'It'll have to wait. If the ACC wants me to catch Swainson's killer I'd better keep at it. Thanks for your help, Peter.' The two men shook hands and the doctor left.

'We ran a credit rating on Dr Ingham, sir,' Johnson said, as Alec settled at his desk. 'It's in the tray. And the personal file, which came through this morning from the other hospital.'

Alec leafed through the papers in the tray. 'Good work. When Dr Ingham turns up, don't rush to bring him through. Just let me know he's here.'

He turned to the personal file as the door shut behind the constable. In cryptic form, it sketched the career which had already been analysed so damningly by Dr Pritti. Ingham's degree was good, rather than outstanding. He had proceeded through the normal sequence of hospital jobs up to registrar level, which he had reached at the lateish age of thirty-four, probably, Alec surmised as he flicked through the papers, as a result of taking a few wrong turnings on the way to his decision to specialize in haematology. There was then a space of four years in which Dr Ingham laboured to gain his postgraduate exams, succeeding at the third attempt. Simultaneously there was a period of absence, amounting to some four months in all, on unspecified compassionate grounds. By then, Roger Ingham was thirty-eight, and his appointment as senior registrar at the new district general hospital must have seemed all the more welcome for coming so late. Then nothing. Yearly increments and pay awards. A certain amount of sick leave, generous but hardly inordinate. Annual assessments, completed by Swainson, that damned with faint praise. 'Eminently suited to continue in his present post' was, Alec mused, about as final a death sentence as you could have on your career. At the very end of the file, a handwritten memorandum recorded Dr Ingham's temporary appointment as locum consultant.

The credit search was revealing. Dr Ingham and his wife carried a mortgage which must have been at the very limit of what the building society would advance on his salary, and might even have been influenced by reassurances of future promotions. Then there were hire purchase charges in favour of several well-known retailers, presumably for carpets and furnishings. There was even, Alec was interested to see, a standing order to pay off solicitors' fees on the house purchase. It began to look as if Dr Ingham's financial affairs were not merely pressing but positively overwhelming.

The phone rang and Johnson announced that Ingham had arrived. 'Give me five minutes,' Alec said, 'then I'll be free to see him.'

He swivelled his chair so that he could look out of the window. For once, there was no little procession wending its way along the paths, just a man and a girl chatting in the middle distance. He thought the man was Dr Pritti. Could the girl be Mary? He saw her laugh and turn away, while the man raised his hand in farewell. Webs of relationships. Had Dr Swainson been aware of the web at the centre of which he sat? Some of it was of his own spinning, after all. He must have known of Ingham's ambitions, frustrated in part by his own presence. Perhaps he knew how little his colleagues felt for him as a man – was it a personal sense of worthlessness which drove him to the domesticity of his affairs? It was, after all, the lukewarmness of people's reactions to Swainson which worried Alec most. With the possible exception of Ann Ringer's retrospective hate, the emotions Swainson had evoked were pitiful in their coolness. None of the women with whom he had any relationship, his wife included, seemed to have truly loved him. So far as a murder investigation was concerned, Alec would have felt much happier with some evidence of genuine passion, jealousy or guilt. Once again he found himself pitying a man whose death could cause so little sense of loss.

'Ask Dr Ingham to come through,' he said.

Roger Ingham began, characteristically, with bluster and unconvincing authority, and Alec's heart sank at the prospect of dealing with such a clumsy adversary.

'I really do take exception to be dragged over here only to wait around. You seem to have no understanding at all of the demands on a doctor's time. Now that I have the extra responsibilities of a consultant it is even more inconvenient that I should have to come all the way over here for some piffling query that could have been cleared up over the phone. I should have insisted that you came to see me instead.'

'Yes,' agreed Alec mildly, 'you should.'

Dr Ingham's mouth clamped shut and he seemed undecided whether or not to take Alec's reply as an impertinence. Alec waited.

'What is it, then?' Ingham asked ungraciously.

'In the first instance, Dr Ingham, perhaps I could run through with you again the question of your whereabouts last Saturday.'

'I've already been over that. Why can't you listen properly? You should have made notes. I told you . . .'

'Yes, Doctor, I recall what you told me, and I agree with you on the advisability of notes. What worries me are the discrepancies between what you told me, as recorded in my notes here – ' he pushed his notebook slightly towards Dr Ingham with his pen – 'and what in fact happened. Could you run through things again?'

Dr Ingham frowned. 'I . . . it's a long time ago. You

don't record everything while you do it on the offchance that someone is going to ask you about it later. What sort of discrepancies, anyway?'

Alec shook his head. 'Come now, Doctor. That's not the way to approach it. Let's start again. You got up at . . . '

'I don't know. Nine.'

'And you spent the morning . . . '

'Reading the paper. Doing some odd jobs in the house.'

'You said in the garden, when I asked you last time.'

'All right, in the garden. I was in and out. You know how it is with domestic chores. Then we had lunch. And went shopping.'

'Leaving the house at what time, approximately?'

'Half past twelve, one o'clock, something like that. We went to –'

'Half past twelve or one o'clock. Not later? If I said you didn't leave till two, what would you say?'

'All right, it might have been two, I don't know. If you're doubting whether we went –'

'Half past twelve or one o'clock, or it could have been as late as two. Not earlier, anyhow? You couldn't have gone out before lunch? What time did you eat, as a matter of interest?'

'How the hell can I remember that? No . . . yes, it might have been earlier, I suppose. Perhaps twelve. How can I answer your questions when I don't know what you want me to say?'

'Quite,' Alec said. 'Only if you went out earlier than twelve, presumably you either had lunch out or did without it altogether. Does that seem likely? The later time, up to two o'clock, would seem more probable, I should have thought.'

'Yes, yes, I suppose you're right. I really don't see that

you could expect us to record all these details at the time. Why should we?'

'Why indeed? Now, as to the visit to the DIY supermarket. We've followed that one up because of course a store like that keeps copies of receipts. We indentified the right one from a list of the things you bought. Mrs Ingham kindly supplied us with that.'

Dr Ingham flushed. 'You've no right to trouble her with this. She's not in good health and I try to take as much strain from her as I can.'

Alec looked at him, realizing he was sincere for once, and was sobered.

'I'm sorry we had to do that. The receipt, of course, proves that you did go to the store as you said. I'm content on that score, so that's something we can agree on, anyway.'

'I'm glad to hear it. In that case, why waste my time discussing it?'

'And we agreed that twelve was the earliest you might have left the house, though one or two was more likely.'

'Yes, but –'

'You must have a very fast car, Dr Ingham. To leave the house at twelve and be buying goods in a DIY store eight miles away at eleven-twenty-four.'

Ingham's expression became hunted, the unconvincing mask of authority crumbling into the face of a man sure of nothing but his own misery.

'I wasn't there that early.'

'You should have looked at the receipt more closely, Doctor. It's got the date on it, hasn't it?'

'Yes, that's the whole point.'

'Not the whole point. It also has the time. You really didn't notice that? Oh yes, it's got the time on. I expect you'd been to that store before and when you wanted a way of proving where you were on Saturday morning, to show you weren't at Ovenden, you remembered that the receipts were unusually detailed. So you and your wife drove out to the store on Saturday morning together, but you didn't go in. You left her there, didn't you, Doctor, to wander round and buy half a dozen small items after giving you time to drive to Ovenden, so that when you were challenged, you'd have a till receipt to show that you were six miles away buying screws and adhesive when all the time you were at Ovenden in the mortuary meeting Dr Swainson, weren't you? Weren't you, Doctor?'

'There's a flaw in your reasoning, Inspector,' Ingham said. 'If I went to all that trouble to arrange an alibi, don't you think I would have used it?'

'I think you intended to, if need be. But I think the alibi was set up for some other purpose than to cover a murder – something where investigation might be less thorough. Dr Swainson's death made it too risky to use. You're clever enough, Dr Ingham, to appreciate that it is sometimes better not to have an alibi, especially one which can be broken down with a little trouble. So you met Dr Swainson for some purpose which was serious enough to make an alibi worthwhile but, at least in intention, less serious than murder. What was it?'

'I never met him,' said Ingham.

'Take care, Doctor. Think before you speak.'

'I never met him. I intended to, I admit. We'd made an appointment to meet to . . . to discuss a professional matter.'

'What was it?'

'I can't tell you that. It was a professional matter, I couldn't discuss it with you.'

'You normally meet in the mortuary to discuss your patients?'

'He had to go there anyway. To sign a crem form. The

point is, he never showed up. I never met him last Saturday.'

'How were you going to get in?'

'He'd be there, he'd let me in.'

'But when you arrived the door was open and you walked in.'

'No, it was locked, he never showed up. I waited till twenty past – we'd arranged to meet at eleven – then I left. The next thing I heard on Monday was that he was dead.'

'Leaving you to step into his shoes as consultant. And into his salary. That must have been a welcome piece of news, mustn't it? To a man pressed for money?'

'How can you say that? My God, you're saying I killed him so that I'd profit by it.'

'Come now, Dr Ingham, the histrionics are really unnecessary. You've known all the time we must suspect you. Mysterious assignation in the mortuary, the very place Swainson's body was found, the motive and the knowledge to do the deed. Are you really so shocked?'

'You've no right,' Dr Ingham said illogically. 'You can't talk to me like that. I suppose you want to charge me. If so, I want my solicitor.' He sat up in his chair with an attempt at self-possession. 'Kindly get me an outside line.'

Alec ignored his request. 'I'm not going to charge you, at least, not yet. And if your solicitor were here, I'm sure his advice would be to tell the truth instead of peeling off layers of lies like the skins of an onion with always a new one beneath. This appointment with Dr Swainson – it was to discuss a patient, you say?'

'I didn't say that. I said it was a professional matter.'

'But you felt it necessary to hide the fact from us that you'd arranged to meet. More important, you felt it necessary to provide yourself in advance with an alibi.

Doesn't that sound like carrying professional discretion a little far?'

'It wasn't an alibi. You called it that, not me. I merely dropped my wife off to do a little shopping while I came on to see Dr Swainson.' Ingham was recovering his poise, and his customary haughty, resentful look was creeping back.

'You still say it was a professional matter?'

'Yes.'

'Dr Ingham,' Alec said sweetly, 'you are telling me another lie. I know you are. You know you are.'

'Prove it.'

'I shall.'

'Do you think he was the blackmailer, sir?' asked WPC Simmonds after Ingham had gone.

'He might be, after all it was a pretty poor attempt at blackmail, from what we know, wasn't it? It would mean he got his wife to telephone Margaret Bickerstaff – she said it was a woman's voice, remember. I doubt if he would have got anywhere with Swainson himself. Are people so afraid of being known to be unfaithful these days?'

'But if he'd found out something new, he might have another try.'

'Mm. Whether for cash, or more likely for Swainson's resignation and his own nomination as his successor.'

'And then he met Swainson and they couldn't agree terms, and Ingham did away with him.'

'Possibly. Tempting, isn't it? But there are too many things that don't fit. Well, it's time I headed off to Angela Norman's boyfriend. Wonder why he rang us? See you in the morning.'

'All right, sir. Take care.'

Alec looked at her sharply, then suddenly relaxed and grinned. 'And you,' he said, and went out in lighter heart.

Alec, face to face at last with the reserved Dr Norman's confidant, found himself strangely reluctant to open the conversation. John Steadman was both older and more grave than Alec had anticipated and the room they sat in might be the model for the old-fashioned solicitors' office in countless films of the 'fifties. Dusty box files and law books lined sagging shelves in mahogany bookcases, and the air itself seemed heavy with precedent and tradition. Steadman himself dressed for the part of the reliable family solicitor, but there was a shrewdness in his gaze which cautioned against a hurried and casual approach.

The older man watched him with a gravity in which there was also a hint of understanding of Alec's discomfiture.

'Let me make your task somewhat easier, Inspector. I know what has happened to Geoffrey Swainson, of course. I may view it from a different angle to you, since I learnt of it from someone whom it has affected very seriously. I know, too, that you must entertain very considerable suspicion about Dr Norman. That may or may not be justified. I hope to God it is not, and I think it is not. Nevertheless, I want to give you what help I can to enable you to understand something of the character and background of Angela Norman. I have her permission to do so – ' he smiled gently – 'and I hope it will at least encourage you to approach her with some degree of sympathy and understanding.'

'That's very good of you. You say you had Dr Norman's sanction for this approach. Would you have made it if you didn't have her approval?'

Steadman stared through the window at the distant hills, shadowed by rain. 'Perhaps. I'm glad to say the situation doesn't arise. Was it Waugh who remarked that given a choice between betraying his country or betraying his friend, he hoped he would have the courage to betray his country? I have never been happy with that proposition. Sometimes my friends may have thought me unfeeling for thinking that even friendship can be outweighed.' He turned to Alec sadly. 'I have known Angela many years. Am I wrong to want those who are investigating her husband's death to be successful?'

'But you believe her innocent of his death,' Alec said.

'I hope her to be. I don't believe, these days, if I can help it. What do you want me to tell you?'

'Could you just talk? About how you came to know her, how well, when you meet and why, what you talk about. What she was like when you first met, what she is like now. If you would?'

John Steadman leant forward and poured more coffee for them both, and stayed bowed over the tray, stirring absently at his cup.

'I've known Angela a long time. From when she was a child. I don't suppose you can imagine her as a small girl, Inspector. But to me, it's more strange to see her as a mature woman in her forties, in the middle of a career. I knew her mother well, you see. In time, when it became obvious to us that there was no future between us, I became a friend of the family and a sort of honorary uncle to the children. A harmless friend who would remember birthdays and come for dinner every few months. And whom Sarah – Angela's mother – could turn to occasionally, when she wanted a shoulder to cry on or advice from someone who would not make the wrong demands on her.'

'You never married,' Alec said simply.

'No, I preferred what I had, and if I'd married I'd have had to give it up. Besides, I suppose I didn't try. In these days of many partners and loose ties it must seem anachronistic to be faithful to a woman you have never married. Anyway, that's beside the point. It's relevant only in so far as it explains why Angela came to see me as a sort of extra relative. She's independent, you know that, of course. I expect you realize that the root of that is loneliness, as it so often is.

'Angela had an elder brother, Inspector. A clever young man, and very winning, too. So much of his parents' love and effort went into his upbringing and his future that there was perhaps not quite enough left for Angela. When he was seventeen, they showed their love tangibly when they bought him his first car. They weren't very bright about things like that. It wasn't a new car, and it was before the days of MOT tests. So they bought a car which was shiny on the outside and rotten within and when Rob was showing off to his friends one evening, as he was bound to do, something snapped and he hit a tree. Angela was almost sixteen then.

'Rob lived for another six years, the years in which Angela decided to become a doctor and began her studies at university. Then he finally died. You see, all the time she was growing up there was this brother winning all the attention, then when she finally started to achieve herself – they weren't a conspicuously intelligent family and she worked hard – her parents were too taken up with looking after their invalid, and then too taken up with their loss, to notice.'

'But she came to you.'

Steadman looked up thoughtfully. 'Yes. She used me to try out her ideas, to test the reactions of an adult. "Shall I become a doctor, Uncle John? Do you think I ought to try? I thought I might." When she got the letter telling her she was accepted for medical school she brought it to show me. Did you know she was quite a competent cellist? Student concerts, she used to invite me to those and I used to go and enjoy them. Well, she wasn't a star pupil, but good, she worked hard. You'll have found out much of this, I suppose, from reading files?'

'A little. Tell me about her marriage.'

'Her marriage. She came to me about that, too. Geoffrey Swainson was at Ovenden when she first went there, and soon she was coming to see me and telling me about this attractive young doctor who was pursuing her. I worried a little, you know, what he was after, as one does. She hadn't really been serious about anyone before. She was far from ignorant, of course; after all, she was a doctor; but that doesn't stop you getting hurt, does it? It wasn't long before she was asking me whether she should move in with him. He had asked her to, but she was undecided. I advised her not to: if he really cared for her he could accept her decision and take the other path, engagement and so forth, and that would be better than accepting something less in the short term. I don't know whether I was right. I thought I was at the time. I still think with most people . . . because of course, they did get married. That's when I began to wonder if I'd been so wise after all.'

'He treated her badly?'

'Depends on your standards. She stopped work, of course. That was her idea. If she was going to be married, she would do it properly, and in any case she couldn't work if she was to have children. I fancy Geoffrey was lukewarm about her stopping work. Two incomes . . . he must have looked forward to being in easy circumstances. Be that as it may, she drew the line at starting a family. I don't think they had much of a married life in that sense, the sexual sense, after that.'

'And he began to seek elsewhere for his pleasures?'

'That was hard to accept. Angela was much like her

mother, and I loved her mother. It was hard to see her turned from. I don't think he'd have married Angela, you know, if he'd given it any real thought. I think it was only because she refused to live with him. Anyway, when he realized how things were he merely started to live as if he was still single. I think he expected her to be quite enthusiastic about such a civilized arrangement.

'She changed, then. I saw her youth disappear all in a few months. She stopped coming to see me at first, sealed herself off as if she wanted no one's care any more and would fend for herself. Well, I wouldn't have that, but it's true that we were never able to be so open afterwards. It was as if a wound had healed over with scar tissue. I don't say that to excuse her. It's just what happened.'

'Has she had affairs herself, since that time?'

'I don't think so. Possibly she may have had brief, one-night affairs, but I doubt even that. She hasn't a very high opinion of men, you know.'

'She might use them to meet her needs, none the less.'

'She might. If she was involved emotionally, if she had become fond of someone, I think I should have known. Perhaps I deceive myself.'

Alec looked at the elderly solicitor with compassion, as he sat hunched forward in his chair apologizing for the decencies he embodied and which he felt to be out of date. A man who had accepted a solitary life because the woman he loved had married elsewhere, who allowed the label of honorary uncle to be tied round his neck like the bell round the neck of a harmless neutered tom-cat, yet a man who preserved his own dignity.

Alec pulled his thoughts together and looked about him, noting the neatness of the papers and books on the desk, the lack of photographs, the small oil of a local landscape on the wall which was the only adornment of the room.

'And you last saw Dr Norman when?'

'The day before yesterday.'

'Of course. And before that?'

'Oh, not for several months. May, would it have been? April, perhaps.' He leafed through a desk diary. 'April the twenty-third. Shakespeare's birthday. I doubt if that influenced our choice of date. We went for lunch in town here. I always used to treat her, when she was younger. Now we take it in turns to be host.'

'Did you notice any difference in her, in her attitude to her husband, anything like that?'

'No. She neither carried a meat cleaver nor mouthed foul threats,' the solicitor said drily. 'I would have asked after Geoffrey, as I always do. I imagine Angela gave her usual reply, though I really don't recall. We talked of holidays, of a little exhibition I was planning to visit that afternoon at the local gallery. I expect I inquired after her work, and she inquired after my health. That would be the normal pattern.'

'If Dr Norman had been premeditating the death of her husband – and I'm being blunt with you, Mr Steadman – do you think you would have been aware of it? Would she drop hints?'

The older man hesitated, then shook his head and sat back in his chair.

'I don't think so. She wouldn't be one of those who feel a compulsion to share their crimes. She would simply ensure that every eventuality was covered and proceed with the business as she would any piece of clinical work. It's a horrible thing to have to say, but it's true, I'm afraid.'

'So you think she might have done this?'

The solicitor looked sadly at Alec as if sorry for him. 'I think she would have been capable of carrying it out if she once decided on it. But I think she would be unlikely to choose such a course of action. Why should she, after all? After so long?'

'Why, indeed?' Alec echoed.

'Would you like some more coffee? I believe there is some still.'

Steadman filled their cups, and Alec said, 'Dr Norman came to see you, and that followed my visit to her. Did she come for comfort? Advice?'

'Not to confess, anyway,' the solicitor said drily. 'Nor to consult me professionally, or I shouldn't be talking to you like this. She came for advice, yes, in the way she often used to, and to let off steam, of course. She was pretty much incensed with your treatment of her.'

'But she didn't ask you, for example, what her rights were or whether there was someone she could complain to? Did you suggest you and I should meet, or did she?'

'That was my suggestion. At least, I asked for Angela's permission to ask you over for a chat and she agreed.'

'Gladly?'

'She agreed.'

'Are you, in fact, her solicitor?'

'No, I am not.'

'That must pain you somewhat. She consults you but doesn't trust you with her affairs.'

'I think she would see it as a reluctance to burden me with them. She chooses to keep our relationship something like what it was when she was young, when of course she didn't have a solicitor at all. I am happy with that.'

Alec rose. 'I think I ought to leave you to your work, Mr Steadman. Thank you for being so frank. What you've told me gives me a better understanding of Dr Norman and that's most useful.'

'It doesn't help you to know who killed her husband, does it? You and I both know, Inspector, that a person's murderer is as likely as not a member of their immediate family.'

'That is often the case,' Alec said steadily. 'But not always. Would you like me to keep you in touch?'

'No, I don't think so. If I'm needed, of course . . . but otherwise I'm not specially keen to hear all the details.'

They shook hands, Alec nodding his thanks, the other man gazing back with slightly faded, but clear-sighted, eyes.

The sunlight struck brightly, despite the late hour, as Alec emerged from the dark corridor, and he strode briskly away, leaving his car where it stood by the pavement. For twenty minutes he marched smartly through the streets and alleys of the old town, across the park, along the river bank with its neat borders and low railings. When eventually he returned to his car he unlocked it without a glance at the dark stonework of the building beyond, and getting in, quickly started up and pulled away.

For the first time, he thought of Angela Norman with sympathy, and if the interview had achieved nothing more, it had been worth the journey to Oxfordshire for that. In the loneliness of her family, where all the hopes, all the care and all the compassion were expended on her brother, she had been thrown back upon her own determination to achieve. Was it any wonder if she had emerged so dauntingly self-reliant and chill? And if she had invested in Geoffrey Swainson all the love, and all the hunger for love, which she had so long suppressed, only to see it regarded as worthless currency – how much more determinedly must she have barred the door on her vulnerability. *Tout comprendre, c'est tout pardonner*, thought Alec wryly. But in this case I am a long way still from understanding everything, and when I do, it is not for me to pardon. I have no authority to do that.

* * *

The flat was dark and cheerless when Alec pushed open the door. It was just after ten, and from one of the other flats the muted tones of the television news drifted up the stairwell. In the big living-room, and in the bedroom, the curtains were undrawn, the windows staring blackly like sightless eyes. Alec pulled them to and took off his jacket, hanging it carefully in the wardrobe. A pair of slacks and the shoes Diana wore for work lay where they had fallen on the bedroom floor and Alec pushed them to one side with the edge of his foot.

In the kitchen, a pan on the stove held a generous helping of bolognese sauce; Alec felt the side of the pan and turned the electric ring on. He wandered around disconnectedly, assembling a plate and cutlery, setting water on to boil for the spaghetti, leaning against the table as he waited for it to boil. He wondered what John Steadman was doing, and smiled wryly as he pictured him following just such a bachelor ritual in his own house, setting the single place at the table and probably propping the paper, or a book, before it, as he would day in, day out, and thinking, no doubt, each time he did so, of how it might have been different and how some other hand might have set his meal before him.

Only later, as he washed up his plate and mug and cutlery did Alec wonder where Diana might be. He sat reading absently until the murmur of the television in the flat below ceased and the church clock struck midnight in notes that swelled and died on the breeze. Should he leave a note about the ACC's party invitation? But it looked unlikely that they would be able to go, for he could hardly leave a murder investigation to run itself, and surely could hardly be expected to. The invitation was a polite gesture of encouragement and favour and Alec made a mental note to decline it tomorrow in properly appreciative terms.

Much later he half surfaced from sleep as Diana came in and shed her clothes quickly on the floor. He heard the gurgling of taps in the bathroom and then the bed dipped as she snuggled up to him. The church clock struck the quarter in four measured notes that lingered on the night-time stillness.

Chapter Eleven

WPC Simmonds came in and sat down.

'All right,' Alec said encouragingly. 'Tell me how you got on with Dr Shepherd.'

'Well, sir, one of the other girls asked me back to the doctors' mess for coffee. Then she had to leave and I stayed on just to see what would turn up.'

'And Dr Shepherd turned up?'

'Yes, sir. Well, we got chatting and I brought things round to the investigation fairly easily. I said that we were beginning to feel we knew Dr Swainson quite well, even though none of us had ever met him. Then I said, "You met him, what did you think of him," or something like that, and took it from there.'

'I can't see Dr Shepherd and Dr Swainson getting on too well.'

'They didn't. She knew of his reputation, of course, or pretty soon found out about it, and that wouldn't endear him to her. She's rather committed to the idea that women are perpetually at risk of exploitation by men, and of course Swainson only seemed to reinforce that idea. There was he, a consultant, having affairs with juniors and paramedics, like a sultan choosing partners from his harem; at least, that was how she put it. The fact that it was as much the partners' choice as his was rather overlooked. Then she saw him discarding each of them as soon as he had had his fill, as if they were Victorian fallen women being cast into the gutter. She knew about Lindsey Welch's broken marriage, and though she doesn't much approve of marriage as an institution, it was pretty good evidence of Swainson's poisonous touch.

'I think she was rather disappointed that nothing similar happened to Margaret Bickerstaff, but she got out of that one with some remarks about the false crutch of religious faith.' WPC Simmonds smiled. 'She rather seemed to be eating her cake and having it over that one.'

'Surely it was before her time anyway?' Alec put in.

'She seemed to know all about it, none the less. Anyway, that brought us to Ann Ringer. You were right, by the way. Whether there ever was any physical relationship between them, there's no doubt that Harriet Shepherd is pretty smitten on the other girl. Ann Ringer embodies every virtue, so far as Dr Shepherd is concerned, not the least of which is the fact that she has been hard done by at the hands of a man.

'Well, sir, I'm afraid I rather strung her along here, saying how scandalous it was that a man like Swainson could do these things and get away with it, and Dr Shepherd said she agreed, and in fact, she'd set out to make sure that Swainson had his obligations brought home to him. I said surely there was nothing much one could do about it, and she said you could at least make sure everyone knew about it.'

'I should have thought there were few people unaware of Swainson's goings-on, in any event.'

'Yes. And it's a funny idea that you express your friendship for someone by publishing the fact that she's been given a sexual disease by her lover.'

'She was going to make that public?'

'Well, I don't know, to be honest. She certainly knew about it.'

'So what did she do?'

'Nothing, in the event, sir. Swainson's death forestalled her. What she intended to do was have it out with him, as she called it. Tax him with his crimes. I don't know what she really thought she'd achieve. She's so naïve, really, sir, you want to tell her she's being her own worst enemy.'

'It's not the sort of attitude that'll bring her much success in her career.'

'She's in the wrong job anyway. She's not much of a doctor, according to general opinion. Well, the upshot is, that she knew he – Swainson – was going over to the mortuary to do the cremation form on Florence Timms on Saturday morning, and chose that as the time to do her angel of conscience act. She spent a good deal of Saturday morning hanging around within sight of the mortuary waiting for Dr Swainson to show up.'

'She didn't go in?'

'No key.'

'And she didn't see him?'

'On the contrary, she did. And he wasn't the only one she saw. She also saw Dr Ingham. And Dr Norman. At that point, I thought I'd better have a word with you before going any further, sir.'

'Ah, Jayne, my sweet, you are a very clever girl. I fancy I ought to have a word with Dr Shepherd. You'd better keep out of it this time, in case we want you to play the sympathetic fellow woman later. Ask Andy to get hold of her directly, will you?'

'And so, from about half past ten onwards you were within sight of the mortuary. Where were you exactly, all that time?'

Harriet Shepherd sighed and took her bitten finger from her mouth. 'In the old laundry building. It looks across at the mortuary.'

'A little boring, wasn't it, sitting there just waiting?'

'You can't help people without some effort. I don't just ignore my friends when they're having a bad time.'

'Did Dr Ringer ask for your help?'

'She wouldn't. She's not the sort to go complaining to others about how she's been treated.' There was a note of proprietorial pride in Dr Shepherd's voice. Alec could well believe that the friendship had verged on the obsessive, on one side at least.

'Tell me what you saw.'

She shrugged unbecomingly. 'Well, I waited a while. Twenty minutes, maybe. I knew he was going to come. He had the crem form to do on Flo Timms. He showed up about eleven.'

'And you went on watching.'

'Not intentionally. I left the laundry when I saw him, but when I got out on to the path where I could see along to the mortuary again, there was Roger Ingham from the DGH just going in.'

'Did he use a key?'

'Not that I saw. He just seemed to push the door as if it was already open.'

'But he might have been let in by Dr Swainson?'

'He might. He could have knocked while I was letting myself out of the laundry.'

'So what did you do then?'

'Went back to the laundry to wait for him to come out. I wanted to see Dr Swainson on his own.'

'You might have waited a long time.'

'I might. In the event, it was about fifteen minutes, I suppose.'

'You're a very patient person, Dr Shepherd. Or very committed to your friend.'

Harriet Shepherd scowled.

'So you saw Dr Ingham come out again about eleven-fifteen. Did he shut the door after him?'

'I don't know. You couldn't see, from so far away. He pulled it to, but whether it was still on the latch you couldn't tell.'

'And then?'

'Then I waited a minute or two, to give him time to get clear. Then someone else came.' She paused.

'That someone being . . . ?'

'Dr Norman. Swainson's wife. She seemed to be in a hell of a hurry, tearing along the path with her coat flapping. She knocked on the door, then pushed it open. Half a minute later she came out again, slipped the catch – I saw her do it – and pulled the door to behind her.'

'When you say half a minute, how long was she actually inside?'

Another shrug. 'Not long.'

'One minute? Five? Ten?'

'Two or three maybe, not more. So I left it a minute or two longer, then I went and tried the door. It was shut, of course, so I knocked. There was no reply.'

'Might he simply not have heard you? If he was in the inner room?'

'Obviously. Or he could have slipped out while I was leaving the laundry, when the mortuary was out of sight, if he'd been smart about it.'

'Is that what you think he did?'

'I thought he'd deliberately decided not to open the door, if you must know. Thought he'd seen me coming. It would be like him to ignore you.'

Alec wondered whether that was true, or true perhaps only for Dr Shepherd. To a man like Swainson, sensitive to the messages of sexual availability, Harriet Shepherd's attitudes would have been unattractive even if her person were more seductive. Perhaps he might have done himself a favour by making a pass at her none the less. An expression of interest, mild flattery, might have shifted the chip from her shoulder to some extent.

'So there you are, outside the mortuary, having failed in your endeavour to see Dr Swainson and reprove him for his misdoings.'

'It's all very well for you,' Dr Shepherd snapped. 'I doubt if you have the remotest concept of standing by your friends.'

'I assure you,' Alec said quietly, 'I was not making fun of you. But you had failed, hadn't you? Did you then give up?'

'Yes. If he was in there, he wasn't going to open the door. I thought I'd have to find some other time to get him on his own.'

'So you went back to the doctors' mess, or your own flat, or where?'

'The ward, actually. I had some things to see to there.'

Where you should have been all morning, Alec thought.

Dr Ingham was not pleased at being called back to Ovenden, but when he was given the option of meeting instead at the police station, he grudgingly agreed. When he came in, Alec wasted no time.

'When you went to the mortuary on Saturday morning, Dr Ingham, you went in. What did you see?'

'Nothing. Swainson never showed up.'

'But you did go in.'

'I never said that. You can't say I said that.'

'Dr Ingham, what you said is beside the point. The fact is that you did go into the mortuary on Saturday morning. What did you see?'

'Are you calling me a liar?' Dr Ingham's face was red.

'If necessary, yes, Doctor,' Alec said quietly. 'You were seen.'

The fight went out of Dr Ingham with uncanny speed and he slumped in his chair. 'You're trying it on,' he said dully. 'There wasn't anyone.'

'You mean you didn't see anyone. If it comes to it, Dr Ingham, this witness – ' he dwelt with slight emphasis on the word – 'will testify that you went into the mortuary. You may have been the last person to see Dr Swainson alive.'

'Except the murderer.'

Alec just looked at him. At last he said, 'You'll have to tell me the whole story, Dr Ingham. You can see how it looks.'

'You haven't charged me,' Ingham said with a flash of his old truculence. 'You haven't said all that about not having to say anything, and writing it all down.'

'No, I haven't charged you. Whether I do depends on what you tell me now, and whether I judge it to be true. You see, you may convince me of your innocence. I say, you may.'

Alec turned away and gazed out of the window. Outside in a bush a blackbird began to sing, loudly and liquidly. It cocked its head and regarded Alec as Ingham began to talk.

'I could have killed him. I had the opportunity and by God he gave me enough motive. But I didn't. I wouldn't, I never would, I don't like death. I wouldn't bring death to anyone before their time. He wasn't a pleasant man, he'll be no great loss. There're other people in his line just as good, even if they don't spend all their time at conferences and whatnot. He hated me, you know.' He looked up at Alec, then down again at the desk. 'No, that's too strong. Swainson never felt any emotion as strong as hate in his life. He disliked me. I'm a good doctor, though I say it myself. Ask anyone. But Swainson wouldn't have that. He knew I was never going to get to the top while he stayed in post and he took delight in the fact. He took delight in being well off, in having his big house and never having to watch the money. He knew we had to, that we'd pushed ourselves to the limit and then been caught by the rise in interest rates. And he resented . . . it seems odd, but he resented the fact that Julia and I love each other. Maybe he once loved his wife, I don't know. I know he never felt love for the pathetic string of women he slept with. I think he felt that as his loss and it made him more set against me.

'Why did I go to see him that Saturday? Because of the blackmail.'

'I know,' Alec said. 'You had been blackmailing his mistresses, hadn't you? And he'd found out.'

Ingham looked startled. 'Is that what you . . . ? Oh God, you think it was me.'

'Wasn't it?'

'No. I'd never do that.'

'You were in financial straits. You had the opportunity and the motive. And if not you, then who was it, Dr Ingham?'

'So you're beaten, Inspector?' A little, surprising smile played briefly round Ingham's mouth. 'You're asking me who it was?'

'Yes, I'm asking you.'

'It was Angela Norman. That's why I went to see him. I knew, oh yes, she'd tried it before. On Margaret Bickerstaff, on that other girl, Lynn something. She'd have tried it on Ann Ringer except that the girl had been to her clinic and I suppose she drew the line at that. Then she tried it on Josephine Carmel, and we decided that something would have to be done. He'd have to be stopped,' he said simply. 'Oh, not stopped in the way you mean, Inspector.

'You know about Jo, of course. She came to Ovenden

with a conviction for defrauding her previous employer. I don't know if she'd done it, maybe she had. Anyway, she came here because the local MP took a fancy to her and took her case up. What I do know is that she's done a miracle here. You don't understand what it's been like in the Health Service these last few years. Well, she's taken Ovenden forward, when every other hospital in the region has gone backwards. If she had any debt to society, she's worked it off, Inspector, believe me. Angela would have undone all that. She didn't go for money, that's not why she did it, she just liked making them squirm. They were all women, you see, and they had all enjoyed something with her husband that she hadn't enjoyed for years, or she thought they had. She would have broken Jo just for the pleasure of it, as a child pulls the wings off an insect, and with as little compunction.'

'How did you know all this?'

'Jo told us. She comes to us quite often. She doesn't have many friends, you see. Then it came out that she was trying it on her, too. So I fixed with Geoffrey to see him on Saturday morning. To give him a taste of his own medicine. Either he stopped Angela, or I blew the gaff.'

'Don't you think you were being remarkably stupid, Dr Ingham? Did you really think you could improve matters by a move like that? He'd just turn it back on you and say you were smearing him because you were jealous of his job.'

Dr Ingham hesitated. 'I didn't think of it, not before I went. Then when I talked to him he was . . . he was distant and superior. It was bloody humiliating,' he said with sudden force. 'He said he knew I had a grudge against him because of my career not being what it might but he hadn't realized I'd go to such lengths to take his place. He made it quite plain that he would get in first and that his word would be listened to before mine.' He looked up at Alec. 'I was naïve. I realize that.'

'I think you were, Doctor. So you went to the mortuary. Who let you in?'

'Geoffrey did. I knocked on the door and he came and opened it. We talked for ten minutes or so. As you've described. He told me to go away and think about it. Supercilious, he was, laughing up his sleeve. He hadn't a scrap of concern for Jo or for any of them,' Dr Ingham burst out angrily. 'That's what really got me. He just didn't care.'

'And then?'

'I left.'

'Pulling the door to?'

'I don't . . . yes. Geoffrey had put it on the latch when he let me in, and I just pulled it to behind me. Then I went back and picked Julia up from the DIY store. That was it, till Monday. Then I heard he was dead, and I was glad. I'm sorry, Inspector, but I was. I suppose I realized, too, that I'd be top of the list of suspects before long. I didn't kill him, though.'

Alec leant back in his chair and stared out of the window and thought.

Alec pushed Johnson's latest report away from him with the end of his pencil and then, just in case, covered it up with some other papers before returning his gaze to Angela Norman.

'You told me earlier that you and your husband made love on Friday night. In fact, our specialist tells me that almost certainly isn't the case.'

'I don't see how he can possibly know one way or the other.'

'Nevertheless, that's what he says. You told me a lie?'

'Yes. I wanted to protect the silly girl's reputation. I

knew about my husband's goings-on, Inspector, and I put up with them. But I draw the line at handing over his victims to be torn to pieces by you people.'

'You fail to convince me, Doctor. I know you tried to blackmail at least one of your husband's mistresses. That doesn't sound much like compassion for them.'

Angela Norman's eyes narrowed. 'Who told you that? It isn't true, I need hardly say.'

'Never you mind where we learnt it.'

'It matters a great deal. If it was someone with a grudge against me, for example.'

'You knew there had been blackmail, though. How could you know if you were not behind it?'

'How could I know?' she laughed derisively. 'Don't try these policeman's tricks, Inspector. You haven't the style. Everybody knew about it, and who was doing it. The same person that told you, I've no doubt. Roger Ingham. I took you for a fool, Inspector, but not so much of a fool as this. Roger Ingham bungles everything he touches, and he bungled the blackmailing like everything else. That's why no one did anything about it, until Geoffrey decided it would have to stop. He was going to have it out with Roger. You've been taken in, Inspector.'

She laughed again and Alec sat clenching his teeth, trying to remain cold and unflurried and wondering if he had perhaps been the great fool Dr Norman thought him.

'Go away and do your homework, Inspector, before you come bluffing your way with me. I'm surprised they let you loose on this matter, I really am. How wrong I was to get upset with your questions just because I thought them offensive. They were merely incompetent. I'd have done better to laugh in your face.'

Alec took a grip on himself. 'You lied about another matter, Dr Norman.'

'Be careful what you say, Inspector. You may be

incompetent, but if you start to use words like "lie" to me I shall stop laughing at you and begin to take steps that'll do you no good at all.'

'On Saturday morning, you say you tried to contact your husband but you didn't see him. He wasn't to be found, that's what you told me.'

'Yes.'

'But that, too, was a lie, Dr Norman. He was in the mortuary, as you knew he would be, and when you went to him there you were seen.'

Her face grew harsh, ugly, and the elegant body, the attractive figure, clashed angrily with her expression and lost their charm.

'If Ingham says that he's lying and you're a fool to believe him.'

'Possibly he didn't see you – he hasn't claimed that he did, though you probably passed each other on your way to the mortuary. How did you let yourself in?'

'I didn't . . .' she stopped.

'Tell the truth, for heaven's sake,' Alec said sharply; then, more gently, 'it would be better, you know.'

'It was on the latch,' she said sullenly.

'You did go to the mortuary, then.'

'Yes. I thought my husband might have been there, someone said he had a crem form to sign. He wasn't.'

'It's a long way from your clinic, Doctor.'

'I had a patient not turn up so I went to fetch some papers from medical records. It's on the way, Inspector, as I've no doubt you know.'

'Why were you looking for your husband?'

'To tell him about . . . to remind him about going out that evening.'

'But he wasn't there.'

'As I said.'

'So you left. Leaving the door open?'

'No, I shut it properly. It shouldn't be open when there's no one there, so I slipped the catch and pulled it to.'

'Didn't you think someone might have been working there and just left it on the latch while they slipped out for something and then been unable to get back in because you'd locked it?'

'More fool them. They'd have had to get the key from reception and open it again.'

'Or from the secretary's room.'

'Not after . . .' she stopped.

'Yes, Doctor. Not after . . . ?'

'Nothing.'

Alec changed his approach. 'We found threads of a surgical glove by Dr Swainson's body. You would use such gloves in your clinic, of course.'

'Many people in this hospital would use them.'

'But not, for example, Dr Ingham.'

'He might get hold of a pair if he was planning to commit a crime. To avoid leaving fingerprints.'

'He'd be taking a risk, then. Surgical gloves are rather too fine.'

Was it fancy, or did her cheeks turn a little paler?

'If you have fingerprints you should be able to find the person who killed my husband.'

'Oh, I don't see any difficulty in doing that.'

'But you haven't made an arrest.'

'I like to have as much as possible tidied up first. After all, we do know when Dr Swainson died, and we now know how. Until today, I didn't know for sure how he came to be in the mortuary drawer. Now I think I know even that.'

'You think he was already dead when I went into the mortuary? That's a horrible thought.'

'I find the alternative less pleasant. Tell me, Doctor,

was there anything lying around when you went in? No papers? No crem form half filled in?' She shook her head. 'No keys?'

'I didn't search the place. I simply looked in to see if my husband was there or not.'

'You see, Dr Norman, whoever disposed of your husband had a certain amount of intelligence. They realized that if everything was removed from the scene of the crime it would be harder to work out when and how he died. The crem form, for instance: if he had been writing that when he was attacked, or whatever, it might be blotted where the pen had slipped. It might even be that the surface of the desk below would be torn where the pen had dug into it as Dr Swainson slumped forward. Of course, the criminal might overlook that, or at least be unable to do anything about it.

'Then there was the question of the keys. Dr Swainson had a key to get in. Now, my guess, Dr Norman, for what it is worth, is that after so many years at Ovenden, your husband had acquired his own keys to many of the buildings, and that it was his own key he used to get into the mortuary on Saturday. However, if this key was removed, the issue would be clouded. It would be confused even more if a key from the office of the woman with whom he was having an affair was left in its place.

'You wouldn't worry about the implications for Miss Carmel. She had already had one brush with the law, so one needn't be too scrupulous about involving her in another.

'As it happens, your husband had a chance, a very slim chance of surviving his ordeal, because there was another visitor to the mortuary on Saturday morning. Unfortunately, that visitor either came in the short interval when your husband was still unconscious, or was unable to hear his frantic attempts to extricate himself from the mortuary drawer.'

'This is fantastic, Inspector,' Dr Norman exclaimed. 'You seriously suggest he was already in the drawer when I went into the mortuary and I knew nothing about it?'

'No, I don't suggest that. I suggest that when you went into the mortuary your husband was not in that refrigerated drawer. When you came out, he was.'

'I want the telephone. I want my lawyer.'

'You shall have him,' Alec moved the phone towards her, but she continued speaking.

'How am I supposed to have got him into the drawer? Knocked him out or something? It's fantastic and impertinent. And it's a fabrication. You don't know what happened to my husband and you dream up some impossible story just to get yourself off the hook.'

'Not impossible. Merely improbable. Given a certain chain of coincidences, not even that.'

'You can't prove it was me, Inspector. It could have been Roger, or Jo Carmel. You may think I killed my husband, but you have to convince a jury that I did. I think your senior officers will tell you that you haven't a case.'

'I think I have, Doctor. Oh yes, a lot of it is circumstantial, I agree. You were in the mortuary on Saturday morning – as I say, you were seen there. You went over to take your husband the fresh bottle of Epilim tablets, didn't you? He ran out on Friday night – we've worked that out for ourselves by calculating the daily dosage from the number of tablets in a bottle. I don't think that worried you much: you got to know your husband after he'd settled into the Epilim routine and the dosage had been stabilized, so you've probably never known him have a fit. Dr Swainson, on the other hand, was more anxious, and rang you on Saturday morning to make quite sure you remembered to go to the chemist's for a fresh prescription. We know from the chemist's records – ' he touched the papers briefly with his fingertips – 'that you did in fact do that, but my guess is that you got back to the hospital too late to do more than make a cursory attempt at getting hold of your husband. But he was becoming worried, sufficiently so to ring you at eleven-twenty and arrange for you to bring the Epilim over to him in the mortuary. So you went over there. I think, actually, you had no idea of killing your husband at all at that stage. But when you went in, you found he was right to have been anxious about his pills. Did you find him unconscious, or did he have the fit while you were there? Anyway, it was the final coincidence which tipped the balance for you. He was writing out the crem form. Had he left the drawer open while he did so, the drawer with Florence Timms in it? Is that what gave you the idea? Because, suddenly, you realized that you needn't put up with your husband any more. The boredom, the humilia-tion, and the final indignity of believing – wrongly – that he was a herpes carrier: you didn't have to put up with these any longer. The idea flashed into your mind and you carried it out, it was as simple as that. You slipped the pen back into Dr Swainson's pocket, and you probably thought quickly enough to look for the empty Epilim bottle and remove it. Then you pulled him over to the bank of fridges. There was some risk, for you knew he would be unconscious for no more than a minute or two at most, but you might be able to talk your way out of it if he woke. You laid him in the bottom left-hand drawer and you simply pushed it to. I think the murder would have pleased you. No fuss, no violence. But it was just as effective as shooting him. Just laying a living man down on a hard bed and sliding the drawer shut. Easy.'

Alec turned in his chair so that he could gaze out of the window. Dr Norman sat impassively.

'I think he had probably left the key on the desk beside him,' Alec mused, 'and when you took the crem form you noticed the key and took that also. It was too risky, after all, to open the drawer and put it in your husband's pocket. He might be conscious by now and even you would have difficulty in explaining what he was doing in the mortuary fridge. Later, of course, you realized that you could secure your position by leaving the key from the secretary's room in the mortuary for us to find. We would assume that she had given it to him on Friday night, and when you told us a really beautiful lie about having sex with your husband on Friday night, knowing we would recognize it for a lie and draw the false conclusion that he had spent the night elsewhere, the finger of suspicion would point firmly at Miss Carmel. Obviously, they had spent the night together and quar-relled, and obviously she had followed him to the mortu-ary on Saturday morning and done away with him there. After all, she was a woman with a record, and far the likeliest suspect for a murder.

'Was it on Saturday night or on Sunday that you slipped Miss Carmel's office keys from the keyboard at reception, let yourself in and took her mortuary key? Then you took it over to the mortuary where you dropped it beside the table for us to find. You can hardly be blamed for overlooking the fact that the grass had been cut by then, even though that simple fact may prove to be the final knot in our case. I think your husband was already dead by then. I hope he was. It would worry me to think he might have heard you return and know that you could ignore his agony. I shouldn't like to think quite so badly of you as that.'

'It's an interesting hypothesis,' Dr Norman said after a

while. 'Of course, I deny every word. It's the sort of fantastic explanation a young detective on his first murder case might come up with in his enthusiasm. I fancy he would think better of it when he had time to consider.' She looked at her watch. 'I think I had better leave you. I have a clinic in ten minutes.'

Alec rose politely. 'Would you be ready to come to the police station afterwards, please. Could we say about three? Fantastic though the theory may be, there are certain formalities I have to go through with you, if you would be so good. Meanwhile, WPC Simmonds will accompany you to the clinic and wait while you see your patients, and I shall have a look through your house. I do have a warrant. Of course, we may not find what we're looking for, but there's usually something. You'd be amazed at the evidence even quite careful people leave behind, and how little it takes to convince a jury.'

After Dr Norman had left, Alec spoke on the telephone to the superintendent at county headquarters, and then, briefly, to the ACC. He put the phone down and sat staring at it for several minutes. Then, reluctantly, he picked it up again and dialled John Steadman's number.

Chapter Twelve

Alec returned to the flat to find Diana already there, and in a bad mood. She had received his call that afternoon about the party with disbelief. She had had a full day at work, including an acrimonious exchange with a man whose unwelcome attentions she had been repulsing for three months and who had chosen this day of all days to become abusive. She had the prospect of a similar day, with similar problems, tomorrow. The new evening dress she had treated herself to only ten days ago was in the wash, and as a result she would have to wear the same outfit she had worn to every party for the last three years, and the shoes that went with it were scuffed. She was two days into her period and all in all was feeling at her least attractive, her least amiable and her least able to cope. By the time Alec made his late entrance general discontent had hardened and sharpened and needed only an outlet to explode in anger or tears.

The explosion, when it came, was decisive. Alec, for once dull to the subtleties of Diana's moods, failed to perceive what was in the offing and said little to her as he pottered about putting on a suit and a change of linen. When Diana, who had been sitting at the dressing-table in a slip applying make-up, took her dress off its hanger to put on, he was unwise enough to say, 'I thought you decided you'd over-exposed that dress recently?'

'Of course it's over-exposed. I've nothing else to wear, have I?'

'What about the cream one you bought the other week?'

'It's in the wash. If you won't give me more than a few hours' notice of the bloody party you'll have to put up with me looking terrible. Take someone else if you don't like it.'

'I only said – '

'Oh, just piss off, will you, Alec? I know what you said. You don't have to repeat it.' Diana turned away angrily while Alec stood irresolutely by the bed.

'Have you had a bad day?' he asked eventually.

'What do you care?' Her shoulders were tense, the voice stifled, and Alec knew she was crying and didn't want him to see.

'I'm sorry about the short notice,' he said reasonably. 'If it's any comfort, it's a hell of a nuisance to me, too. I've had to leave Johnson and WPC Simmonds to carry on without me, and you know how I hate asking others to work after I've left.'

No reply. Alec shrugged and carried on getting ready.

'You're not worried because of who's going to be there?' he asked after a moment.

'No. Why should I be?'

'You are sometimes. Used to be,' he corrected himself. 'There's no need. They're only ordinary people who've happened to be fairly successful at what they do. Some of them not even that, just born into a successful family. Most of them are pretty dull. Come on, Di, you know you're a match for any of them.'

'In a dress I've worn at every party for the last three years. Not going as me at all, just as a companion for Inspector Stainton. You'll be bloody charming to everyone, as usual, and I'll be the odd one out. I don't think I'll go.'

'Cut it out,' Alec snapped. 'You said yes, and I've accepted on your behalf. If you really want to look stupid, all right, stay at home. But just stop moaning for once.'

Diana snatched angrily at a tissue from the box on the dressing-table and began furiously mopping at her make-up.

'What're you doing?'

'Taking this stupid make-up off. If I'm not coming, I won't need it and it's all smudged anyway.'

'Look, Di,' Alec sighed, trying to regain control, 'I want you to come. You know it won't be any fun without you. Not that it'll be much fun anyway. There's no one else I'd take even if I could.' A fleeting thought of Jayne Simmonds in a long evening dress darted unbidden into his mind, and he hastily suppressed it. 'We've got to go, and we've only got forty minutes before we have to be there.'

In the end, they drove to the ACC's house in prickly silence, unreconciled. Diana clenched her teeth and resisted the temptation to inspect in the vanity mirror the make-up she had reapplied over her tear-stained face. It would be obvious she had been crying, she knew. Well, damn them all, let them notice. Just don't let anyone make a comment or ask if she was all right, or they'd get a response they didn't bargain for. Beside her, Alec's conservative grey suit and regimental tie seemed to emphasize the sharp good looks of the archetypal well-bred young officer. He would be easy in tonight's company, she knew, however tired or bad-tempered he might be inside, making conversation with practised civility and well-mannered interest, whether to the Chief Constable, his ultimate boss, or some titled matron. Or a glamorous deb, Diana thought. There were always a few of those at these do's and they usually homed in on Alec like hounds at the kill, and with much the same glint in their eye. She was tempted to make a scene, show him up in some way, assert her own personality by shocking or being ill-mannered. She sighed. It would hardly be fair, and would do nothing for her self-respect.

Besides, whatever the interest of the debs and their mothers and their well-heeled fathers, it was she, Diana, who was with Alec tonight. It was she who had the sharing of his flat, and his bed. Let them think of that, and if they showed signs of overlooking it, well, she would just have to jog their memories for them. Rather more cheerfully, she settled in her seat and crossed her legs.

The Assistant Chief Constable's house was an attractive affair in local brick which couched discreetly behind tall hedges in a private road. It had the deceptive spaciousness of the older family house and Alec wondered if private money had aided its acquisition. Nowadays, these houses changed hands for sums that even the most exalted policeman could hardly afford.

A maid, hired for the evening, took their coats and ushered them into a drawing-room that extended the depth of the house to open French windows at the far end. The room was already half full and guests had spilled out on to the terrace. Alec saw at once that they were a well-judged mixture. If the middle-aged predominated, there were yet sufficient younger guests to keep some sort of balance, while there were also two or three very elderly people whom Alec marked down to talk to later. In his experience, it was likely to be a worthwhile pleasure.

With practised ease the ACC spotted their arrival, excused himself from his immediate circle and with his wife came to greet them. In a domestic setting he seemed rather more authoritative than in the bustling police HQ and he welcomed Diana by name with mannered courtesy, and Alec with familiarity.

'Glad you could come. I'm pleased with developments in your case today. It's good of you to make the time. Still, I'm a great believer in mixing some pleasure in with one's hard work. You haven't met my wife. Daphne, you've heard me mention Alec Stainton, and this is Diana. Perhaps you've bumped into each other at the university?'

Daphne smiled and explained that she worked as a counsellor for problem-ridden students. Soon she and Diana were chatting easily about mutual acquaintances and the ACC – 'call me Jack for this evening' – led Alec off to a knot of men at the far end of the room. Soon he was chatting busily with Peter and the local coroner. The ACC wandered off to meet fresh arrivals, and in due course brought them over to Alec's group, accompanied by Diana.

'You know Angus and Bella, I believe, Alec. Can I leave you together? I'll try and get a word myself later.' He melted away again, intent on his duties as host.

Angus said, 'I say, Alec, you really seem to be the man of the moment tonight, old boy. I gather you've solved the Case of the Frozen Consultant. Rather expected you to be wearing a deerstalker and smoking shag in an old meerschaum, as a matter of fact.'

Alec grinned. 'It's not as bad as that, but thanks all the same. Have you met Diana? This is Angus Mitchell. We know each other from playing soldiers. Don't let the dim army type impression deceive you – it's entirely genuine. And this is Bella, about whom World War Three almost got started when we were in Berlin one time.'

The two girls smiled reservedly at each other. Bella was indeed strikingly beautiful, and Diana felt her guard coming up.

'Lovely to meet you, my dear,' Angus said emphatically, staring deliberately at Diana's breasts. She flushed and half raised a hand to cover her low neckline, whereupon Angus smiled contentedly and raised his eyes mockingly to hers. She smiled back, rather guardedly.

'Alec always did have a way with delightful girls, though

he had a distressing tendency to like them to be intelligent as well. I'm sorry to see he's been able to lead such a lovely young woman as yourself astray.'

'Are you sure it was that way round?' Diana asked.

Angus's eyes opened wider. 'After all these years wondering how to spell *femme fatale*, have I actually met one? Try your skills on me, please, I beg you.'

Diana found they had somehow got separated from the rest of the group, and decided to change the subject.

'You knew Alec when he was in the army?'

'For my sins.'

'He never says much about those days.'

'Could it be because he's ashamed of spending his days playing childish mess-games and sipping duty-free gin?'

'Was he good at mess-games?'

'One of the best. And I speak as no mean practitioner myself. He was good at other games, too. The tougher sort, where it doesn't pay to lose. Believe me, Alec could have gone right to the top.'

'I thought he was only a captain when he came out?'

Angus shook his head. 'Doesn't matter. He was tipped for great things. For a start, Staff College were begging him to honour them with a visit, and I've no doubt he'd have had a spell as an instructor there too. He was a really good soldier, Alec, and it's a tragedy he didn't stay in. Though he doesn't seem to be a failure exactly at police work. You're a lucky girl, Diana, believe me.'

'Thank you. It's nice to be told.'

'Mind you, I don't know that I'd fancy cuddling up to someone who's killed quite so many people, if I was in your shoes. Be a bit of an acquired taste, I should think.'

'You mean Alec has? I can't believe that's true. I thought soldiers didn't get to kill anyone in this country these days.'

Angus frowned. 'Most of us don't, thank God. Or

unfortunately, depending on whether you look on the matter as a theologian or as a question of training. But you know about Alec's undercover stuff, of course. There has to be quite a handful who do things like that – none of us know quite how many. Mostly in Ulster.'

It was Diana's turn to frown. 'He never told me he was involved in anything like that.'

'Good for him. He's not supposed to talk about it, of course, not to anyone, but I always fancied everyone had to tell someone.'

'You mean, he worked in plain clothes? As a sort of army detective?'

'Sort of.' Angus stared into his empty glass, discomfited and wishing they had not embarked on the topic.

'But he also killed people.'

'Well, yes, I suppose so. I'm guessing. Perhaps he didn't, I may be wrong.'

'So he worked in plain clothes for the army in some sort of undercover job that involved killing people?'

'Not innocent people, after all, Diana.'

'Oh?'

'Well, if they'd been innocent, he wouldn't have had to . . . oh God, ask him yourself.'

'I will. So these people had been tried and convicted?'

'Not exactly.'

'And there were none of the little accidents that we hear of occasionally on the news, mistaken identity, men who unaccountably weren't carrying guns after all, women caught in the cross fire, none of those?'

'Oh, sod it. Look.' He held her eyes soberly. 'People do these jobs. It's to Alec's credit that he did it well, very well, and that he was happy to leave it. He's a good man, whatever he may have done, and I don't say that lightly. Now let me get you another drink and we'll each find someone else to talk to. Don't let it spoil the party, Diana.'

'I wouldn't dream of it.'

'He's obviously done rather well with this murder inquiry,' Angus said more lightly. 'He must be on course to the top, I should think.'

'Thank you. Actually, I have a career of my own which I find at least as absorbing as Alec's. Believe it or not, it brings me as much satisfaction, too.'

'All right. Point taken. You don't like me much, and I'm not sure the feeling isn't mutual. That doesn't make what I've said any less true. Let's get that drink.'

For Alec, it was a pleasant party while it lasted. He was content to see Diana chatting away to Angus, and the general standard of conversation was high. An agreeable selection of punches and fruit cups refreshed, while attractive not-too-insubstantial titbits tempted the appetite. In due course he found himself free to circulate, keeping half an eye cocked to rescue Diana if she showed signs of being neglected or unpleasantly besieged, and soon he sat down beside a delightful old lady who flirted becomingly and released snippets of scandalous gossip about the other guests. When she was joined on the other side by a great-niece in an off-the-shoulder dress that showed off a good deal of very attractive bosom and slim legs, Alec began to feel that this was really a very pleasant party. Discreet congratulations flowed from unexpected directions and his inner glow at the effective conclusion of the case kept the underlying exhaustion at bay.

Nevertheless, he was happy to fall in with Diana's suggestion soon after ten that they make their excuses and leave. His own energies were flagging, but he was shocked to see just how drawn Diana looked. Clearly he had underestimated the strains of her day. They made polite farewells and left.

Later, Diana sat by their bedroom window in her dressing-gown while Alec tugged at his tie.

'Did she kill her husband?' she asked suddenly.

Alec started at the unexpectedness of the question. 'Yes, I think she did.'

Diana stared out of the window at the dark lawn. 'You don't know,' she said. 'You don't really know whether she's guilty or not. You've merely found a reason to close your file.'

'You can't argue like that. How can you ever know one hundred per cent that anyone's guilty? Everything works on the balance of probabilities. Anyway, it's not my problem now. I don't decide whether or not she's guilty, thank God. The jury does. Let it be, Diana, love. I've had enough of it tonight. Come to bed.'

'No.' She sat in the half dark staring out over the lawn. With the inside lights off, the window had ceased to be a black mirror and became again a window, on to a shadowed landscape where minute contours were raised to hills by the low moon. A cat stalked slowly across the grass, king of this unpeopled country.

'It's late.'

'I'm thinking.'

'Do it tomorrow.'

'I must do it now.'

'That's silly. After a party when you're tired isn't the time for thinking. And you've work in the morning.'

'You go to sleep. I'll come when I'm ready, maybe.'

Alec, with sudden premonition, watched the unmoving silhouette, chin on hand, the features hidden in shadow. The figure moved as she turned her head.

'I'm thinking whether or not to leave.'

The words hit Alec like a fist and robbed him of speech. Like an actor improvising a scene, he tried on his tongue the possible responses and found none he could utter with conviction. Yet something had to be said, lest he seem merely indifferent.

'Please don't,' he said at last. And then, 'Why now?'

Diana turned to the window again. 'Why now?' she mused. 'It may as well be now. Because in the long term it has to come, and knowing that, I'd rather it was now. I couldn't cope, you see. Not with the things you did when you were in the army, not with the things you still do to make yourself a better policeman. You've chosen with your eyes open to accept those things. Well, my eyes are open now, and I can't follow you.'

'I didn't want you to,' said Alec, and the remembrance of the ghosts he struggled alone with in the dark times was strong. Since Diana's coming the ghosts had been weaker, and he had been more at peace. 'I tried to keep it from you.'

'Yes. And that's the final reason, Alec.' The silhouette changed as Diana turned again and stared at him as if trying to read something in his face in the darkness. Then she turned away again. 'I can't explain any more.'

'But I need you. I love you,' Alec said, and cursed himself for sounding melodramatic.

'It's sweet of you to say so, Alec. I think you may even believe it. But it isn't true. You'd find that out in a while. I'd rather be gone before you do.'

'You're not trying to decide, are you?' he said, aggrieved. 'You've already made up your mind.'

A pause. 'Yes.' Alec, watching her profile dark against the window, thought her shoulders shook as if she were crying, though no sound came.

Suddenly, harshly, the telephone rang. As if in a dream, Alec lifted the receiver and gave the number.

He listened in silence for a moment, his eyes on Diana, hers on him, then replaced the receiver.

'That was the ACC's son,' he said thinly. 'I have to go back there. Something's happened but he wouldn't say what.' They gazed at each other for a long moment, then Diana nodded and dropped her eyes, and Alec reached for his clothes.

It was well past midnight and the streets were empty and clean beneath the sodium lamps. Cars were still scattered outside the ACC's house. Alec knocked and a young man with a serious face opened the door.

'Would you mind joining my father in the study, please? Thank you for being so prompt.'

Peter and the coroner were already in the small study, together with the Superintendent and the ACC.

'Glad you could join us, Alec,' the ACC said gravely. 'I'm afraid there's been a bit of an accident. It seems to support our view of the case, but it's regrettable none the less.'

'Hardly an accident, sir,' the Superintendent said bluntly.

'You're right, of course. It's Angela Norman, Alec. It appears she's hanged herself in her cell. We're just going down there now. Will you come?'

It was hardly a request and Alec merely nodded, shocked and sobered.

'I'll just slip and tell my wife,' the ACC said. 'Nobody else need know for the time being. They'll find out soon enough.'

He left, and Alec turned to the Superintendent. 'I'm very sorry this has happened, sir. It's not the way I'd like the case to finish.'

The big man shrugged. 'Was the alternative any better? A sordid trial, the rest of her life in prison?'

'She might have got off. It isn't a watertight case.'

'I wouldn't have wanted that, old son,' the Superintendent said seriously. 'Friend she may have been, though I never knew her that well, but she was guilty of her husband's death. If we had any doubts, we can say goodbye to them now.'

'Do we all have to go?'

'It's best. Get it sorted out straight away. You know the stink it raises when someone dies in custody. It'll be worse with its being a woman, and a doctor, too.'

The ACC returned and they trooped out. The party was not quite over, and the noise of conversation and the chinking of the glasses from the last determined guests mocked them as they argued briefly about cars. There was a moment of bizarre comedy when someone pointed out that they were all over the limit to drive, but the ACC cut quickly through it, coopting his son and the pretty girl Alec had talked with earlier, who turned out to be his niece.

At the police station the ACC asked the two young people to wait and the little procession, incongruous in their formal clothes, mounted the steps.

It didn't take long to hear the story from the desk sergeant, then they trooped down to the cells where an ashen WPC met them and ushered them to the tiny room where Angela Norman had ended her life.

'We took everything off her that we are supposed to, sir,' the WPC said miserably, 'and we looked in on her every half-hour.'

There was an undignified crush at the cell door, and Alec hung back till the two senior men had seen their fill.

'If they want it badly enough, they usually find a way,' the Superintendent said in gruff compassion, and began to shoulder his way along the little passage towards the stairs.

Alec moved forward into the dreary room. Peter rose from beside what had been Dr Angela Norman and met his eyes briefly.

She sat grotesquely propped against the cell wall. Her tights, her belt, even her bra had been taken from her, along with the contents of her pockets when she was first searched, and Alec was unaccountably touched by the grim pathos of her bare legs. Her torso was bare, too, the mottled breasts large and sagging over the creased skin of her stomach. Above, her neck and face were swollen and distorted. The smells of death already filled the room.

Hanging from the bracket of the washbasin was a twisted, damp mass of cloth which Alec recognized with difficulty as the trim silk blouse Dr Norman had worn for their last interview earlier that day.

'No doubt about what she soaked it in,' the doctor said wryly. 'It must have taken some courage, to set about killing herself so deliberately. Was it remorse? Or fear of what the future held?'

'Or just the final expression of her loneliness,' said Alec. He turned away, and as he did so this latest ghost slipped silently into its place in the dim, shadowed recesses of his consciousness. They would meet again.

The visit dragged on in the dreary rituals of administering death, preparing a press release and phoning it through to the papers. In their smoky offices, old hacks raised their noses as the news filtered through from the night desks and sniffed appreciatively at the piquant aroma of scandal.

It was after five when they were done, and later still by the time Alec had collected his car and driven soberly home. The flat was silent. The bedroom door stood open, the room empty, and when Alec turned the handle of the spare room door and pushed it open that too was empty, curtains open, counterpane over the bed. In the kitchen he found a place laid for one, the few plates and mugs from the night before washed and put away. Beside the mat was an envelope. There was no name on the outside, and within just a single sheet of paper, written on one side with Diana's artistic legible script.

I'm sorry if I seem harsh in going away like this. I shall be at my sister's but please don't ring or come and see me if you can help it. I'll collect my things while you are out one day and leave the key. If you were an ordinary constable perhaps it would have worked, but I loved you for being you and now, because of who you are, I have to leave. You have been very kind. I look forward to hearing great things of you.

Beneath were a few lines from a poem they had discovered together when first they met, and had made their own for its astringent tenderness. Alec saw now that it was really, had always been, a valediction. There was no signature, no 'with love', no kisses. He turned from the letter and drew back the curtains. The bleak dawn was already softening into day.

Chapter Thirteen

'Well, that's it,' Alec said. He contemplated the empty desk, the boxes of files on the floor waiting for collection. The telephone sat forlornly on its own, and already the room was regressing to the dustiness and disuse of a week ago. He fancied the very air had begun to smell stale again.

Alec looked at the two constables: Johnson tired but happy, leaning on the back of a chair; Simmonds drawn but still self-possessed, attentive.

'I'm very grateful to you both,' he said formally. 'I expect this case will have taught each of us a lot that will stand us in good stead in the future. I'm mentioning your good work in my report, of course. Jayne, I was going to recommend that you be considered for transfer to the CID. I take it you'd like that. You've been more often out of uniform than in it, these last few days.'

'That's very kind of you, sir. I think I'd like to stay in the uniformed branch, though, if you don't mind.'

Alec felt momentarily pained. 'No, if you'd rather. I just thought . . . I'll go and see the secretary, let her know she can have her office back. Will you just hang on till all our stuff's been collected, then you can go, and many thanks.'

He made his way unhurriedly to Miss Carmel's office. After only a week, the corridors and paths seemed familiar and receptive to him so that he felt a pang at leaving as if he had spent years here rather than days. Perhaps in a place like this, he mused, where it was at first so easy to lose your way, you grew more proprietorial when once you had mastered it.

'Poor Geoffrey,' Miss Carmel said, after she had taken the keys and passes and noted a few practical matters about phone and electricity bills. 'You couldn't say that nothing in his life became him like the leaving of it, for he hated fuss. I suppose you feel you know him pretty well by now.'

'Yes. It's a strange feeling.'

'Does it puzzle you that so many women were ready to be his lover? He damaged our lives for us; oh yes, I know about Lindsey Welch's divorce. I know about Ann Ringer and poor Dr Shepherd . . . Margaret Bickerstaff. But we must have wanted it as well. None of us were "taken advantage of", you know.'

'We all hurt others,' Alec said, thinking of Diana. 'Some of our sins are public, some are not, that's all.'

'Sins? Perhaps. I'm not an expert in theology, Inspector. They've asked me to resign, did you know? Oh, not formally. Just a hint. Didn't they use to leave a loaded pistol on the table for the man who had brought dishonour to the regiment? Anyway, much as they'd hate to lose me, and so forth. I'm thirty-seven, Inspector. You read my file. You know the references I'll get from here.'

Alec shook his head. 'Don't go. Not just to save my guilt, but don't go. They can't sack you, and they won't want to when they think about it. This isn't tragedy, it isn't even news any more. Merely, a man dies. It happens every day. And as for infidelities, affairs . . . a good hospital secretary can't be weighed against them.'

Miss Carmel looked at him uncertainly and a little uncomfortably, and he shook his head again and smiled.

'Wait. At least do that. Three weeks. Then decide, if you're still being pressed. But you won't be. The hospital's lost two people; a third is too much to pay.'

He rose, and she stood also and followed him to the door.

'You've made it easy for us to work here, Miss Carmel. I hope we'll meet again soon.'

He held out his hand. The secretary took it, then stepped closer and, reaching up, kissed him on the cheek.

'I don't suppose many of your suspects do that,' she said. 'This one would like to say thank you to you. I don't deceive myself, Inspector. If I am able to stay on here it'll be because Inspector Stainton was assigned to this case. Goodbye.'

Back in the office the files, the photocopier, all except the desks and telephone had been removed. DC Johnson had gone too, but Alec heard footsteps in the inner room, and when he looked in found Jayne Simmonds gazing out of the window.

'Don't want to leave?' he asked.

She turned and smiled. 'I said I'd wait for the van, so Andy could get off. They've only just gone.'

'Let me buy you a drink,' he said. 'It seems a sort of anticlimax just to push off now. Don't worry, Diana isn't expecting me. To tell the truth, she's – ' He caught himself angrily on the verge of unburdening himself in intolerable self-pity to this uniformed colleague. 'She's away for a while,' he finished firmly.

Jayne considered. 'Would you come for a meal, sir? I'd like to do something special as it's the end of the case, and it'd be nice to have someone to share it with.'

Alec heard the warning bells begin to ring, and opened his mouth to decline.

'I'd like to, that's very kind,' he said formally. 'Only you'll have to promise to stop calling me "sir" if I'm to be your guest.'

She laughed. 'All right. Just for tonight, sir. Will you follow me in your car?'

Jayne Simmonds lived in a terraced house near the centre of town. It was an unpretentious neighbourhood, but Alec guessed there was shrewdness as well as modesty in her choice, for the little houses bore all the signs of impending fashionableness. Her house, inside, was as orderly as she was, but not so reserved, for her books and records, the prints on the walls and the curtains at the window, all gave glimpses of the Jayne Simmonds reserved for off-duty hours. She directed Alec to a tiny bathroom, neat and trim. No tights dried over the bath. No open jars of creams and powders littered the shelves, no half-used packs of tampons lay carelessly shoved in a corner. Alec peeked in at an open door off the tiny landing to see a room laid out as a study, but softened by floor cushions and a teddy-bear propped on the windowsill. The last door was shut, but he saw that it was not quite to, and with a guilty consciousness nudged it open. A bedroom, undefinably feminine though free from frills, with a low single bed with drawers beneath, simple cream walls with two large line drawings, a chest of drawers and a wardrobe. Alec looked for signs of other occupation and found none; a family group in a simple frame on the chest, a snapshot of a cat beside the bed were the only keepsakes on view. That told him little, Alec thought, as he softly pulled the door to. A woman like Jayne would not surrender her privacy to invasion by mementoes of lovers past or present, but it did not prove that that single bed was never shared. He went downstairs, certain his guilty prying must be revealed in his face, to find Jayne pouring boiling water into the teapot in the kitchen, her discarded uniform jacket hung on the back of a chair, the severity of her blouse and skirt mocked by the loosened wisps of hair which she brushed back absently with the back of her hand.

'I expect I ought to offer you a drink,' she said, smiling, 'but I usually prefer to come home to a cup of tea. Terribly domestic, isn't it? Would you like to have a seat while it's brewing and I'll just change into something more comfortable.'

She slipped upstairs, and Alec moved into the living-room. Yielding to a common temptation of his, he crossed to the bookcase and began to scan the titles. It was a habit for which Diana had often reproved him, especially when he indulged it in the presence of his hosts. If he wanted to dissect their psychologies, she said, he should at least wait till they were decently out of the way.

Here, the mixture was interesting, not least for its variety. There was an absence of the more lurid airport paperbacks, but novels were there. So were classics, Austen and Dickens. So was a book of cartoons, and another on Iceland. A commentary on the letter to the Romans lay alongside a collection of poetry of the Second World War. This last he slipped out, and began to leaf through.

'Checking me out?' Jayne had come back downstairs without his hearing her, and peered over his shoulder to see what he had picked out, an amused smile on her face. She had changed into a pair of neat jeans and a bright sweatshirt and released more of her hair from its daytime constraint, and the effect was out of all proportion. Alec found himself running his eyes up and down, taking in the details of her appearance as if they had never met before, while she stood calmly watching him do so, smiling still.

'I always look at people's books first, too,' she said. 'Very rude habit, but you learn a lot.'

Alec slipped the war poets back into their place. 'I'm

always getting told off for doing it,' he said, 'and if, as sometimes, the books are more interesting than the people, I sometimes have to be prised away from the bookshelf lest I neglect to talk to them at all.'

'Stay and read if you like,' she replied, amused. 'I'm only going to put some food on. I'll bring you your cup of tea.'

'All right. Provided you tell me if I can help.'

'Fine. We can talk through the doorway until you get too engrossed.'

Jayne Simmonds seemed to have put off with her uniform her formality with her senior officer, slipping easily into a casual friendliness entirely appropriate to the situation. Alec, who admired this sort of instinctive social skill, found himself in danger of being thoroughly impressed, and felt his own poise melting away to leave him just such a worshipping fan as Jayne encountered by the dozen in the force. He pulled the poetry book out again and settled into a chair, turning the pages until he came to 'Naming of Parts' and settling to read with pleasant familiarity.

'Were you glad it was her?' Jayne called through after a while.

'Dr Norman? If it had to be anyone,' Alec said. 'You couldn't like her, but it's always hard to think our job is to put them away. She was a good doctor.'

'Mm. Would you rather it went unsolved? Rather she didn't pay for her crime?'

'Why should she pay for that one in particular? So many of us never do pay for our crimes, after all. No, I couldn't wish it unsolved, but that's partly just my wish for success in something I'm concerned in. I'm surprised you don't think it hard on her, though. I'd expect you to feel sorry for her.'

'Sorry?' she mused. 'I don't know. Feeling sorry for

someone seems rather a liberty, somehow. If I'm sorry, it's for the whole mess. Ingham, Angela Norman, Miss Carmel, Harriet Shepherd. Us.'

'Us? What on earth for?'

'Oh, just for being part of the whole thing, the mess which produces things like Dr Swainson's murder.'

'For being human.'

'If you like.'

'That's a very gloomy philosophy, isn't it? I think I should have expected something more optimistic from you. You always seem quite content with life.'

'I think I am, in a way. But not content with the way life is, if you know what I mean. How can one be? To be sentimental about life is to be unrealistic. It's messy, and flawed, and full of hurting and damaging. But I enjoy my own life none the less.'

'That sounds an extraordinarily patronizing attitude.'

'I'm sorry,' she said simply. 'You wouldn't like to come and chop some beans, would you?'

Later, after a simple, impressive meal, they sat chatting in the small living-room. The wine they had opened with the meal stood half empty on a low table between them, a window was open on to the diminutive back garden and the evening birdsong drifted in, underlain by the distant hum of traffic. Alec felt relaxed, but weary and a little sad, the results perhaps of the wine. The low table seemed a barrier between them, carefully erected by Jayne to keep the evening under control. She sat with her bare feet tucked up under her, swilling a little wine in the bottom of her glass, thoughtful, attractive, desirable, just out of reach. Alec watched the pulse beat rhythmically in the little hollow at the base of the neck, under the silky skin. The sweatshirt hung softly over her slim body, following the outline of the shallow, wide-apart breasts.

It's time I went, Alec thought. I'm going to spoil this evening if I stay, and spoil the chance of having this girl for a friend. Might it not be unbearable, though, to have her as a friend? Might it not be preferable to risk the outcome and at least have one evening of trying to reach her as a desirable woman? There was no guilt in him about Diana, and he felt ashamed, sure he must be diminished in Jayne's eyes for being so ready to be unfaithful. If only she herself would take the initiative, ask him to stay, break the appalling fetter of friendship and free them to love.

'Poor Alec,' she said. 'You're worn out, aren't you? I should have let you go home to bed.'

He shook his head miserably, looking down at his glass. There was a rustling and she was kneeling at his feet, not submissively, but companionably, resting her folded arms on his knees and gazing up at him.

'If the Super could see us now,' Alec essayed a joke.

'He'd understand. I expect he goes home sometimes, don't you, and Mrs Super comes and sits on his lap. Even Superintendents need to have some time when they're being human.'

'You haven't met the Super's wife, if you can talk about her sitting on his lap. She'd make a Russian weightlifter look skinny.'

'Alec,' she said, and he blinked as she used his Christian name again, 'don't be anxious about Diana going away. I expect she feels she needs time to reassess things. I'm sure she'll come back.'

'I . . . don't know whether I want her back,' Alec said bleakly.

Jayne shook her head violently. 'You can't know, not tonight, with the case still fresh in your mind, and other things to distract you. You've used up your resources on the case, but tomorrow you'll start to build them up again, and then you'll be able to see clearly and know what you want.'

Alec smiled. 'And are you being totally neutral?' He gestured down at her. 'If you mean me to be anxious to have Diana back, shouldn't you be trying a little more convincingly to keep your distance?'

'Yes, I should.'

Silence.

'I'll stay the night,' Alec said, sure it was what she wanted.

'No.'

'You want me to.'

'Yes, in a way. But in another way I don't, and that way's more important.'

'Give the other way a chance for once. It's no great matter.'

'No, Alec. Alec, do you know my nickname at the station?'

'Mm.' He'd heard them refer to her, clumsily, as Baked Alaska.

'Warm and soft on the outside, cold and hard on the inside. You think they're right. That not yielding to one's emotions means they probably don't exist. Yes, you do,' she smiled as Alec shook his head. 'But you're wrong. Oh, I know you're not often wrong, are you? Especially when it comes to assessing people and their motives. You're a good judge of character. But this is something that if you don't know for yourself you'll never understand in others. Only, I think you do know it in yourself. Perhaps not for this issue, but for others. So don't be hurt.' She smiled up at him sadly, fearing his misunderstanding, that he would think the choice she was making was the easier one. She moved, and Alec shifted in his chair, so that she half sat, half knelt in the shelter of his legs, where her arms could reach his waist and he, leaning forward, could take her up in his arms and caress her. She turned her face up to him, and they kissed.

COLLINS CRIME

The Marshal and the Murderer
Magdalen Nabb

The young woman had come to report that her friend was missing. They were both Swiss, teachers; they had come to Florence to learn Italian and stayed on, working illegally. The missing girl had worked as a potter in a small local town and when the Marshal instigated a search there it wasn't long before they found her body.

His inquiries met with suspicion, even hostility, in the inbred, yet deeply divided community with its long memories. Then there were the mysterious wartime tragedies he could get no one to talk about.

Only as the startling truth about the two Swiss girls emerges, intertwining strangely with the bitterness of the past, does the Marshal begin to tie up the ends.

'Hats off once more to strong, cogent Queen Nabb'
Observer

'Bull's eye again! . . . mastery and strength until the last page' Georges Simenon

'Crafted with care. A pleasure to read' *The Times*

COLLINS CRIME

In the Shadow of King's
Nora Kelly

Historian Gillian Adams has returned to King's College, Cambridge at the invitation of Alistair Greenwood, the brilliant, but cold and egotistical Regius Professor. But after she has delivered her lecture and the applause finally fades, Greenwood is dramatically shot dead before her eyes.

As a witness, and as friend of Edward Gisborne, the Scotland Yard detective seconded to the investigation, Gillian is doubly involved, though the quest for Greenwood's murderer promises to be complex - there are so many people with excellent reasons for wishing him dead.

'Enjoyable' *Daily Telegraph*

'Good, strong characters and a well-depicted Cambridge background' *TLS*

'A newcomer of promise' *Guardian*

Fontana Paperbacks
Fiction

Fontana is a leading paperback publisher of both non-fiction, popular and academic, and fiction. Below are some recent fiction titles.

- ☐ FIRST LADY Erin Pizzey £3.95
- ☐ A WOMAN INVOLVED John Gordon Davis £3.95
- ☐ COLD NEW DAWN Ian St James £3.95
- ☐ A CLASS APART Susan Lewis £3.95
- ☐ WEEP NO MORE, MY LADY Mary Higgins Clark £2.95
- ☐ COP OUT R.W. Jones £2.95
- ☐ WOLF'S HEAD J.K. Mayo £2.95
- ☐ GARDEN OF SHADOWS Virginia Andrews £3.50
- ☐ WINGS OF THE WIND Ronald Hardy £3.50
- ☐ SWEET SONGBIRD Teresa Crane £3.95
- ☐ EMMERDALE FARM BOOK 23 James Ferguson £2.95
- ☐ ARMADA Charles Gidley £3.95

You can buy Fontana paperbacks at your local bookshop or newsagent. Or you can order them from Fontana Paperbacks, Cash Sales Department, Box 29, Douglas, Isle of Man. Please send a cheque, postal or money order (not currency) worth the purchase price plus 22p per book for postage (maximum postage required is £3.00 for orders within the UK).

NAME (Block letters) _____

ADDRESS _____

_____

_____